Pict Book Perfection

How to Successfully Write a Picture Book
that Sells to Publishers and Readers

BY AWARD-WINNING AUTHOR
AND CHILDREN'S BOOK PUBLISHER

BROOKE VAN SICKLE

BIBLIOKID
PUBLISHING

CW01431056

Published by BiblioKid Publishing
PO Box 512, Ankeny, IA 50021
www.bibliokidpublishing.com

Second Edition, First Printing
Paperback ISBN: 978-1-965388-08-2
Digital Ebook ISBN: 978-1-965388-09-9

Approximately 85 percent of the world has an idea
for a children's book.
This book is dedicated to those
who do something with that idea.

GET THE WORKBOOK

Complete the Guided Activities as you read the book
using the <u>FREE</u> Companion Workbook.
Download it at JourneytoKidlit.com/PBP-Free-Resources

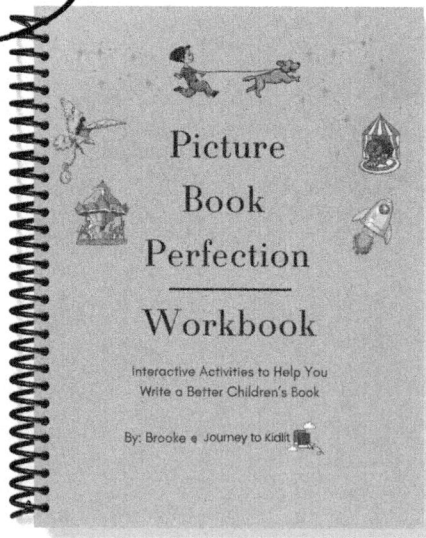

FREE!

Picture
Book
Perfection
———
Workbook

Interactive Activities to Help You
Write a Better Children's Book

By: Brooke • Journey to Kidlit

A Letter From the Author

————◇◇◇◇◇————

IN THE FALL OF 2015, I was sitting at a coffee shop doing some deep soul-searching. I'd been out of college for over three years but was left feeling unfulfilled. Something was missing in my life, and I couldn't figure out what that was until . . .

I read a Bible verse that has become the fuel for which I do everything:

"Speak up for those who cannot speak for themselves."
(Proverbs 31:8, NIV)

As children's book authors, we give a voice to people who otherwise wouldn't get to see their viewpoints expressed in literature. I don't take this power lightly.

After that day, I went to every conference in my area, read every book, and attended every online workshop I could find about children's book writing. I also met a lot of other writers who were like me: writers searching for answers but having no clue where to start.

Writers like you.

This led me to create JourneytoKidlit.com in 2019, an online educational platform that has helped thousands of children's book writers from over 35 different countries find answers on how to write and publish a children's book.

After five years of learning everything I could, I finally saw my publishing dream come true in 2020. I published three picture books that went on to win awards, like Mom's Choice, Distinguished Favorite Preschool Picture Book, and the Moonbeam Award for Best Alphabet Picture Book. Even though 2020 wasn't the *best* year for a book to come out, I was so excited to finally be living the author dream I'd had since I was seven years old.

Maybe that's the same dream that you have for yourself, which is why you picked up this book.

If so, I'm excited you're here!

Before we dive into the book, there are two key things to know:

1. At Journey to Kidlit, we're on a mission to help 100,000 new children's book authors from different backgrounds, experiences, and locations across the world get their stories onto bookshelves in the next ten years.

2. I believe every child deserves to feel seen, heard, and understood in literature. Doing so helps us create kinder, more empathetic communities.

On the following pages, I will share what almost a decade in publishing has taught me, what I've learned about how to create a story that kids love, and the insights I've gained from being a publisher of over 50 children's books.

If you picked up this book because you have an idea for a children's book but aren't sure how to make it a reality, **this book will hold the answers for you.**

I encourage you to read through everything and not skip any sections, even if you already have a manuscript started. And be sure to grab the workbook that goes with this book. (It's free!)

Go to JourneytoKidlit.com/PBP-Free-Resources to get

the free PDF companion workbook so you can implement what you're learning as you read through the book.

Together, I'm going to help you create the very best picture book that kids will ask to read again and again.

Let's get started!

Brooke Van Sickle

Table of Contents

—◦◦◇◦◦—

CHAPTER ONE

Why Picture Books

"To be a successful picture book author, you must read and write A LOT of picture books."

—Brooke Van Sickle

WHEN YOU GOOGLE how many people want to write a children's book, the internet tells you approximately 85 percent of the world has an idea for a story. As someone who teaches about writing children's books, I can attest that almost everyone I know comes to me with an idea they think will make the "perfect" book.

At Journey to Kidlit, we strongly believe every idea deserves a place on a child's bookshelf, but you must write it *well.* (And you actually have to be willing to write and rewrite it.)

That's the difference between you and the rest of the 85 percent who want to write a book—you're actually going to do something about it with this book and the free companion workbook to help.

Like most people who have their first story idea, I set out to write a picture book "for real" in 2015. But books have always been a central point in my life.

I grew up in a small town in Iowa (which is in the middle

of the USA for my international friends). I'm also the second oldest of seven, so reading was the best way for me to get alone time. And we had TONS of books to choose from.

Arthur.

Little Critter.

Sesame Street.

Junie B. Jones.

The Boxcar Kids.

The Babysitter's Club
(*before they were graphic novels*).

And so many more!

I still have my first library card from the field trip my first-grade class went on together. My name is written upside down and everything, but I never wanted to replace it because that's where my love for reading began.

Every weekend, if I wasn't visiting the library, my mom and I would go shopping at Barnes and Noble, and then I would spend my evenings writing stories or journaling about my life. (Let me tell you, reading about things, like how the only ones who remembered my ninth birthday were my cats, gives me so much fuel for my imaginary characters these days.)

But I didn't just want to read the books, I wanted to have the same adventures as the characters.

My brothers and I would spend hours imagining what we would do if we had to live alone in our own railcar, or we'd wander our twelve acres searching for treasure, swinging from random rope swings, and making up stories about the people who lived there before us and left their "junk" yard.

This passion is the same energy I bring to my books, and what I want you to have, too.

This means that no matter what idea you have, you need to tell it in a way that kids will enjoy. In the subsequent chapters, we'll discuss exactly how to do this, but first, you must know what a picture book is.

Writing a Picture Book for Today's Reader

A lot has changed since the 90s, including picture books.

As a young girl, my family and I read every Berenstain Bears, Little Critter, Sesame Street, and Arthur book ever made. But all those books are now 30 or more years old!

The market **has changed a ton** since then.

In the past, picture books included long paragraphs of text on each page, but now, a picture book manuscript shouldn't exceed 1,000 words. And the fewer words, the better! In fact, the word count shouldn't exceed 500 to 600 words if it's a fictional picture book.

This means it is essential to tell a story that is quick and engaging for both the child listening and the parent reading. And remember, picture books are meant to be read out loud. Have fun with your word choice, and don't be afraid to use big or silly words. (We'll talk more about rhythm and pacing, but for now, think: *How can I make this idea something a child will enjoy?*)

Read stories like *Big* by Vashti Harrison (Little Brown, 2023), *Buffalo Fluffalo* by Bess Kalb (Random House, 2024), or *Knight Owl* by Christopher Denise (Christy Ottaviano Books,

2022) to give you an idea of the new style of more recently published picture books.

Understanding the
Different Picture Book Markets

How you publish your book doesn't matter as much as which market you choose to sell your book. The three most popular markets for children's books are the commercial, educational, and gift markets. There are also submarkets that you can sell within these three.

CHILDREN'S BOOK MARKETS

COMMERCIAL	EDUCATIONAL	GIFT
Most Common	Intended for Educational Setting	Intended as Gifts
Primarily Fiction	Primarily NonFiction	Primarily Sensory Stories
Intended for the Masses	Abide by Teaching Standards	Include Pop-Ups Cutouts, Etc.

Commercial Market:

The most common market your book can fall into is the commercial market. These are mainstream books that will appeal to general audiences. Religious and holiday books can also fall into this category if they are fictional.

For the purposes of this book, we will focus primarily on writing for the commercial market since this is the most common market for writers.

Educational Market:

While you might think any book that could apply to schools would fall into the "educational" market, that would be incorrect. Even if you have a book with an educational slant, that doesn't necessarily mean it's a book for the educational market.

For instance, *Pirates Stuck at "C"* (BiblioKid Publishing, 2020) is a picture book that helps introduce the alphabet to preschoolers, but it is not an educational market book. It is a commercial picture book with a concept focused on listing the letters of the alphabet.

The reason it's commercial and not educational is because books intended for the educational market need to be written for the classroom and abide by teaching standards like the Common Core standards we use here in the United States.

If you plan on writing for this market, your book will likely be nonfiction in nature and written specifically with a lesson plan in mind. (Think textbooks, teacher's guides, National Geographic books, etc.) Some great publishers to consider in this category are Benchmark Education, Pearson, and more.

Gift Market:

The final market for kids—the gift market—is the hardest to break into or find a publisher for. Think pop-up books, books with cut-outs, search-and-find, etc.

Because these books are a novelty and cost a lot to produce, many publishers tend to publish fewer titles of these per year or have them produced with their in-house teams. If you plan on self-publishing this type of book, you will likely need to find an offset printing source to help you produce your book since most print-on-demand companies will not offer this type of printing.

Always Write with Your Intended Market in Mind

My first-ever picture book idea was a retelling of Snow White for teenagers between the ages of 12 and 16. Instead of dwarves, I wanted to use sorority girls with body issues to show young girls that not all bodies are created equal.

I was really excited about this idea because it was something that I had wished for as a young child growing up with a lot of self-doubt about my weight and what is an "acceptable" body size. In the early 2000s, it seemed like everyone tuned into the Victoria's Secret show each year, and body image was at the top of everyone's mind.

This made me feel really insecure as a girl, so I thought, *This is something girls need. They need to understand that they're perfect no matter what shape their body is.* And I knew this book was something that was missing in the market.

There was no other retelling like this. All I could think was, *If only I had this as a child, I would have loved it.* And I know that for a lot of you, that's why you might also want to write your own story.

You might be thinking, *If only I had found this while looking for a book on this topic for my child.* Or *if only I'd had this when I was a kid.* That's where many of our ideas come from, which is awesome. It's actually one of the best places to find ideas because we know that there is a reader for it.

But even though I believed in this idea and thought it was something that was really marketable . . .

I didn't realize I **was actually making a major mistake** that many writers make—not understanding my target reader. Yes, I knew who I wanted my target reader to be, which is a great step—you should know that—but I didn't have the correct reader audience for the type of book I was trying to create.

As a children's book writer, you must know who you're writing for. For instance, my published picture books are all commercial fiction, geared for a younger reading audience averaging between 3 to 6 years old (the preschool audience).

You should have a similar idea of who your reader is, too. And be specific!

Things to know about your target reader:

- How old are they?
- What are their parents like?
- What are their interests?

- What similar books exist in the market that they're already reading?

You have to also **understand what they** <u>want</u> in a story.

I was making a big mistake with my first picture book idea because most teens aren't purchasing and reading picture books. Yes, picture books can be read by people of all ages, but when a picture book is marketed and sold, it is typically for readers between the ages of 3 and 8 (and the adults who purchase the books for them). My target reader was not the correct market for that.

You never want to force your target reader to fit into the category just because you want to write it as a picture book. Instead, you should force your writing to fit the correct category for your reader. This meant I should have been writing either an upper-middle-grade novel or an early young adult novel.

When you can make an exception . . .

You might be thinking the same thing I did when I had my story idea: there are exceptions to that rule because there are examples of picture books that are for adults that have sold really well.

This is true.

If you want to make an exception to the standard picture book reader, these are the steps you should take:

- Find examples in the market and note who their intended target reader is.

- Determine why the exception works in this case.

• Decide how and if you can apply that exception to
your book idea.

For instance, if I were to apply these three steps to my
original idea for a picture book, here's how I would do that:

1. Find an example in the market.
Go the F* to Sleep by Adams Mansbach (Akashic
Books, 2011) was an exception I used to justify my
original idea. This book is a picture book geared for an
older target market, except when you think about that
book, it's actually targeting adults who are already
purchasing picture books.

2. Determine why it works.
Go the F* to Sleep is a picture book that's supposed to
be funny for adults. Since the adults who would find
this humorous are already buyers of picture books, this
exception works. But that same situation doesn't really
apply to my idea.

3. Decide if you can apply the exception to your idea.
Could I have figured out how to make my idea
marketable to publishers and agents? Maybe.
But, when you are brand new and trying to get
your first publishing contract, it's best to stick
to the rules as best as you can—unless you have
a large platform or buying audience who will
support your book, like Stephen Colbert did with
Whose Boat Is This Boat? (Simon & Schuster,
2018).

Because while picture books are the most popular category to write for, it's also a category many writers get wrong.

What Does it Mean to Write a "Picture Book"?

The dictionary defines a picture book as a book containing illustrations specifically designed for children. This means that your words and the pictures that will be added later will work together to tell a story.

(Don't worry about the illustrations just yet. We'll get to that chapter later. For now, your job is to focus on telling the best story you can based on your idea.)

While a picture book might have been your first idea, **are you 100 percent sure** that your idea is best suited as a picture book?

If you didn't know . . .

Children's books, which are written for kids between the ages of 0 and 18, are divided into six categories to cover the wide age range. These categories consist of board books, picture books, early readers, chapter books, middle grade novels, and young adult novels.

Since you picked this book up, I assume you have an idea for a story that would be good for kids between the ages of 3 and 8. (That's about the target market for a picture book.) If you have an idea for an older child, it might be a story better suited as a chapter book, middle grade novel, or young adult novel.

Picture books are . . .

Picture books are the most popular type of children's book to write and probably the first category you thought about writing.

They're intended to be read by children between the ages of 3 and 8. (You could simplify this even more and write for ages 3 to 6, 4 to 7, or 5 to 8, depending on who your target reader is.)

Although people of many different ages will read picture books, and teachers may use picture books at many different grade levels, you must keep the intended audience in mind to ensure this is the correct category for your story idea. This is also why most main characters in this category are about six or seven years old—they should be about the same age as the intended audience.

Great examples of recent picture books:

- *Between Two Windows* by Keisha Morris
  (HarperCollins, 2024)

- *Bravo, Anjali!* by Sheetal Sheth
  (Random House, 2024)

- *Built to Last* by Minh Lê
  (Knopf Books for Young Readers, 2024)

- *Penguin Huddle* by Ross Montgomery
  (Walker Books, 2023)

- *There's a Mountain in This Book* by Rachel Elliot
  (Thames & Hudson, 2024)

Now, if you're thinking: *Yes! This is the type of book I want to write.*

Remember, most commercial fiction picture books in today's market are less than 600 words. One of the biggest mistakes I see in picture book submissions today is manuscripts that are over 1,000 words.

When this happens, many authors think they have to change the category for the book to be an early reader, but that's not correct. Because early readers are meant for children to read—most for the first time—they have very specific vocabulary requirements, whereas picture books may have elevated language.

The answer is not to swap your category but to understand how to tell your story with less descriptions and more action. We will talk about this at length in the following chapters, but I just want to prepare you for where we're going.

Your picture book manuscript cannot be longer than 1,000 words in today's world. No child, parent, or publisher wants to sit and read that story.

What if you think your story idea might fit into a different category?

As you begin your writing journey, you may wonder if your idea should be a board book or early reader instead of a picture book. To help you better understand the market, here's a quick breakdown of those two category requirements.

Board Books are . . .

Board books are what we think of as a baby's "first book"

because they're written for children between the ages of 0 to 3. This means they will have very few words. On average, a word count between 0 to 100 words is best for board books.

CATEGORIES FOR READERS

BOARD BOOKS	PICTURE BOOKS	EARLY READERS
Average Age 0-3	Average Age 3-8	Average Age 5-8
Word Count 0-100	Word Count 0-1,000 (Fiction Max 600)	Word Count 1,200-2,500
Mostly Concept Books	Intended to be Read Aloud by an Adult	Intended for Readers Learning to Read (Sight Word Heavy)

As books targeted to infants and toddlers, board books will normally be concept stories. This means they will cover topics like colors, shapes, letters, numbers, etc., to help kids learn basic facts. Although most board books typically don't have a story arc, they will have a common theme or setting that connects the topic together.

Great examples of recent board books:

- *A Bear, A Bee, and a Honey Tree* by Daniel Bernstrom (Hippo Park/Astra, 2024)

- *EidTale: An Eid al-Fitr Adventure* by Aaliya Jaleel (Abrams, 2024)

- *Knock Knock: Who's There?* by Rob Hodgson (Magic Cat, 2024)

- *Make Tracks: Trucks* by Johnny Dyrander (Nosy Crow, 2024)

- *Peekaboo Who?* by Elena Selena (Twirl Books, 2024)

Now, if you're thinking: *Yes! This is the type of book I want to write.*

Consider that board books are a harder market to publish with a traditional publisher due to the cost of production. If you want to write for this market, I would suggest you start with a series idea upfront, as the authors of the *Baby Loves Science* series (Penguin, 2016) and the *ABCs of* series (Sourcebooks, 2018) did.

How to reframe your idea to fit a board book series:

- Narrow down your series "niche."

- Create a story arc to go with your concept.
  (This is also a great way to turn this into a picture book idea, too.)

For example:

Let's say you want to write a book about animals.

- Can you be more specific?

- Are they zoo animals? Maybe even baby animals in the zoo?

- Or even more unique,
  like the most unheard of animals
  in the rainforest from A to Z?

Creating a story concept centered around a narrow focus or topic that hasn't been written about before can make your manuscript more saleable to a publisher.

If you are not familiar with recently published board books, do a quick online search for best-selling board books this year to get a list of examples to check out. Then, make sure to actually read them. Editors can tell when you haven't done your research.

But what if your manuscript ends up longer than the recommended length for a picture book? Should it be an early reader or for an older category of children's books?

Well . . .

Early Readers are . . .

In the first edition of this book, I purposely left the early reader category out. However, in today's self-publishing world, the term "early reader" has been misused in such a mass quantity that I would be doing you an injustice not to mention it.

You see, true "early reader" books are books that kids will first learn to read on their own. This is NOT a fallback for your too-long picture book manuscript. While they have a higher word count than picture books (between 1,200 to 2,500 on average), early readers should mostly use only intentional sight words to help create better, more confident readers.

Great examples of early readers:

- *Dot the Ladybug: The Missing Dot* by Kallie George (HarperCollins, 2024)

- *Flop to the Top!* by Eleanor Davis (TOON Books, 2024)

- *Junior Monster Scouts: Ready-to-Read series* by Joe McGee (Simon Spotlight, 2024)

- *Sketty and Meatball* by Sarah Weeks (HarperCollins, 2024)

- *The Cozy Home* by Ame Dyckman (Beach Lane Books, 2024)

Now, if you're thinking: *Yes! This is the type of book I want to write.*

That's great. Early readers are wonderful stories created with light-hearted themes and normally geared for the educational market.

However, early readers are also a harder market to publish with a traditional publisher. Due to the tightly controlled language and word choice required for these books to be categorized by specific reading levels, most publishers produce these in-house or approach known authors to write these books for them and do not open them to outside submissions.

How to ensure your idea doesn't get too long to be a picture book:

- Make sure you have only one story idea. (Most stories I read that are too long have more than one idea, which doesn't work in a picture book.)

- Remove unnecessary description and dialogue. (We'll discuss how to write in an active voice later, but it's important to remember you will have illustrations that tell part of the story. Not everything should be described in the text itself.)

If you aren't familiar with the existing picture book market, search online for recent traditionally published picture books to get a taste of what readers expect based on your specific story idea. Then go out and read those books!

As a picture book writer, you should read at least ten, if not twenty, traditionally published picture books before you start writing—or even brainstorming—ideas for books to write about. (They're short, so reading them won't take long.)

This will help you understand what readers expect from you as a picture book writer, how other writers approach these types of stories, and what already exists in the marketplace to know if you need to rethink your story idea.

Next, we're going to talk about choosing your story idea and how to know if you have a good idea to write about. Let's go!

ACTION STEP:

Complete the Chapter Activity.

Get the Conduct Your Research worksheet inside the Companion Workbook.

Download it at JourneytoKidlit.com/PBP-Free-Resources if you haven't already.

CHAPTER TWO

Finding a Winning Story Idea

I'VE ALWAYS SEEN books as an approachable way to connect readers with difficult topics—like self-esteem, overcoming fear, promoting kindness, social justice, and more. There are no limits to the kinds of ideas you can explore.

When I was starting out, I came up with an idea for a children's book that stemmed from my experience as a substitute teacher and a very personal memory I had from childhood.

As a teacher, I noticed how students and other teachers would sometimes single out a child for their behavior or how a child would act out based on certain events that piled up. For example, an eight-year-old burst into tears in a P.E. class I was subbing for because he was so stressed. While I wondered what an eight-year-old could possibly be stressed about, these types of incidents brought me back to when I was in third grade.

A boy in my class ran at me full speed and destroyed a diorama I had built for that day's assignment. We both had to go to the principal's office to explain what happened, but I remembered seeing a handful of boys teasing him on the bus about his parents right before he ran into me. Despite my young age, I knew that even though the boy was technically responsible for destroying my project, it was his own internal stress about his family situation and bullying that led to this.

Bullying is the center point of so many children's lives at various times throughout their school years and beyond.

This stirred me to want to create an anti-bullying series for kids. I thought, *What if I could make a whole series of books focusing on different situations, either from the bully's point of view or from a child being bullied?*

SIDE NOTE: If you also have an idea for a series, I wrote a bonus chapter all about picture book series. You can get it for free when you leave a review. Just email me at hello@journeytokidlit.com with a screenshot of your review, and I'll send it to you.

While this series idea didn't become one of my published ideas yet, it was the catalyst for many manuscripts I wrote as I developed my skills as a writer. What about you? What kind of experiences have you had that would make a good idea for a children's book and why is it important for you to write about it?

Where Do Ideas Come From?

If you think about everything that happens in a day, there are a TON of potential ideas you could write about across various genres. But it's our job as writers to sift through those ideas and find the ones that excite us the most. Then, we must decide which ideas we can turn into actual books.

Now, if you're thinking, *But Brooke, where are these amazing ideas that surround me every day?* I say they're literally everywhere!

- At home
- With your family
- In line at the store
- At work
- In nature
- Funny things people say or do
- Online images
- Current events
- Anything that sparks your creativity!

The idea for *Pirates Stuck at "C"* came from the punchline of a joke I read in a *Highlights* magazine. I thought it would make a funny title and stored it in my idea journal for a while. Then, when I was ready to start a new writing exercise, I pulled that idea out and began building an alphabet story from there.

We can all ask ourselves, *What if _____ happened today?* instead of what normally happens. For example, what if the mailman brought a mysterious package to your doorstep with no name or return address? What would you do? Would you open it immediately? What would you find?

Alternatively, you can also try writing popular story ideas from different points of view or from other characters' perspectives.

For instance, if you were to use the fairy tale *Cinderella*, you could write a story from the perspective of the stepmother, stepsisters, fairy godmother, any of the mice, the prince himself, the king, the footman, or even an innocent townsperson who isn't mentioned in the original story. Think about how that would change things!

It's also important for you to become childlike as a picture book writer. Whether that's by building a fort to lie under while you tell ghost stories or watch Disney movies, or by coloring for an hour with crayons or finger paint. Do anything that pulls you away from your adult brain and into the mind of a child.

Think of this as studying for your job. Then do whatever works best for you.

How to Know If You Have a "Good" Idea

Once you have some ideas, it's important to know if they are any good. You don't want to spend a year writing about a specific idea, then another year querying, only to realize that it isn't a marketable idea and that you probably won't be able to sell your story.

Even if you try to self-publish, you most likely won't be able to sell more than a couple hundred copies to family and friends. To avoid this, you need to **do your comp research.**

A "comp book" is a term industry professionals use all the time, and it simply means a book your story idea is comparable to. As a writer, it's your job to know two or three "comp titles" that align with your book idea so an agent or editor can make a connection. By doing your research, you'll actually be able to find out if your idea will be sales-worthy.

How to do your research:

Once you have a new picture book idea you want to write about, start by looking online for similar books. I follow these steps every time I have a new idea:

1. Open up Amazon—or your preferred search engine— and type in the kind of book you're hoping to write. (For example, "Pirate Alphabet Book" or "Pirate Picture Book.")

2. Click to view books that might have a similar feel to your story idea or might even be the same kind of story.

3. Review who the publisher of the book is, the publication date, and anything that might help you know more about the sales data.

NOTE: I like to look at the number of reviews and read the description to see if any major publications reviewed it or if it won any awards. If it's something you've never heard of but has a lot of reviews or the sales ranking on Amazon is high, it's possible it still did relatively well in the market.

Reasons to research:

It's important to do this research before you start writing for two reasons:

1. It helps you know how other books like your idea are selling in the marketplace.

For instance, when I was doing this research for *Pirates Stuck at "C,"* I wanted to know what other kinds of pirate picture books were successful, as well as alphabet books. My book would be competing for shelf space both as a pirate book and as an alphabet book.

2. It helps you know if something similar to your idea has already been published.

When I searched for pirate alphabet books, I found two that already existed in the marketplace: *Shiver Me Letters* by June Sobel (Clarion Books, 2006) and *A Pirate Alphabet: The ABCs of Piracy!* by Anna Butzer (Picture Window, 2016). Before moving forward with my story, I needed to read these books to see how they compared to my idea.

> PRO TIP: To "read" books, I first search YouTube for a book reading of the story. (That way, I don't have to wait for the library to be open or go to a bookstore to find these books.) To do this, simply type "[Book Title] book reading or read aloud." After reviewing the comp books, I then decide how they compare to my story idea.

Completing your research is important because you don't want to start writing a book that already exists in the market, especially if it's been published within the last five, if not ten, years.

For one, publishers and agents won't want to pick it up if they know something similar already exists, and they won't see a need for another story like it. (It won't be able to give them the boost in sales they're looking for.) And two, if you're thinking of self-publishing, it might be hard to sell your story when something like it is already selling well in the market, and you don't have the distribution to compete.

If you find yourself in a situation where something very similar to your book idea already exists, I recommend trying to find a new angle to approach your story from or find another story idea instead. This will help you avoid writing a story that will likely be harder to sell.

Since *Pirates Stuck at "C"* is a physical book, you know those other alphabet books didn't have a similar storyline to my idea. They just happened to be alphabet books with pirates as their main characters. This is great information to know when you begin querying publishers and need to list similar comp books.

Besides having a book that already exists based on your current idea, another sign that you might need to find a new idea is if you can't find ANYTHING else like it. This one is pretty hard to come by, so if you do have this issue, be sure you can justify why there's a need for this book, what target market would want to read it, and why you are the best person to write this story. Without a proven track record, it will be hard to sell an agent or marketing team on why they would want to take a risk on your book, especially if you're a first-time author.

Deciding What Picture Book Idea to Write About

Once you have a few different ideas and have done your comp book research, you need to know how to pick the best idea to write about first. There's a common saying in the writing world that says, "You have to write a lot of bad stories before you'll write a good one." While that is mostly true, I find it's better to be strategic about what ideas you choose to work on. That way, you can limit the number of stories you'll have to write before you write something that's "publishing-worthy."

Here are three ways to know what picture book idea you should choose first:

1. What excites you the most?

As you're working on your story, does this idea keep you up at night? Do you want to write it so badly that you can hardly think of anything else? Choose that idea to start with first because that will help you stay motivated while you're writing. Plus, your excitement will help fuel the story.

2. What is currently selling in the marketplace?

While you don't necessarily want to write to trends because they can have a limited sales window, look for what's already working and write something similar. (Just be sure that you put your unique spin on it.) For instance, if inclusion and kindness is a big seller and you've been thinking about writing a similar story, now might be a good time to finish it and begin querying.

This might also be a good strategy if you're looking to land an agent or a bigger publisher, especially if this topic excites you. (I'm a big proponent of only writing stories you like.) If you're self-publishing, it's important to know what is currently trending so that you can take advantage of people already looking for that kind of story and target them with similar search terms or keywords.

3. What is your overall goal?

Are you trying to land a literary agent? Or do you want to self-publish your stories and have them sold directly to readers? Knowing this will help you to decide how many stories to write each year, what kinds of stories to work on, and what your process looks like from idea generation to finished product.

There is no wrong answer here; you just need to get started! Once you have your first idea, you can move on to the next step: writing your story. In the next chapter, we're going to go over how to do that step-by-step.

ACTION STEP:

Complete the Chapter Activity.

Get the <u>Picture Book Practice</u> worksheet inside the Companion Workbook.

Download it at JourneytoKidlit.com/PBP-Free-Resources if you haven't already.

CHAPTER THREE

"Gathering Your Story Assets"

THE TERM "Gathering Your Story Assets" is the phrase I use when teaching Kidlit Academy students. It means brainstorming your idea fully. This involves knowing your characters, your setting, and your story's purpose.

We'll dive into each of these in detail soon, but first, I want to remind you that each of us has unique life experiences that shape who we are and help us become different storytellers.

For instance, as I mentioned earlier, I'm the second oldest of seven kids and a farm girl. I grew up chasing plastic Sesame Street characters down a creek while wearing mud boots. Since we had so many farm cats, we had a new batch of 30 kittens every six months. And I know just about every type of chicken because we probably raised them at one point or another.

But that's not how my own son is growing up.

The only time he'll ever hug a chicken is at the State Fair, if ever, and instead of having tons of siblings, he'll have neighbor kids to play with and keep him out sledding until ten p.m. on the night of a big snowstorm.

And your experience is unique, too.

Lean into that and use it as a base for your stories. Do you like lyrical or classic storytelling? Are you into folktales? Are you funny? What's your author's voice?

Because I'm a 90s kid, I'm obsessed with all the Disney movies and typically find myself drawn to similar stories or retellings based on my favorite characters, like Cinderella and Snow White.

What about you?

Your unique flair will set your story and your writing apart.

Creating Your Characters

You can probably think of a list of favorite picture books that you loved reading as a kid or ones your kids love to read now. And I bet if we compared our list of books, they would all have this in common: a recognizable character who brings humor, drama, or action to the story.

You need a protagonist in your story who does the same thing, unless you're writing a concept book. This is the person who will have everything happen to them and will directly influence every step of your plot. In nearly all picture books, the main character should be a child or something that represents a child—not an adult.

Since the main character is so important, they can't be as thin as a paper doll. They need to be a full human or human-like animal.

SIDE NOTE: If you plan on creating a series, you must make sure to nail your character. I have a free bonus chapter that explains more. Visit JourneytoKidlit.com/ PBP-Free-Resources to learn how you can get it.)

Even when you start to explain a book you love to a friend,

you probably start by describing the character first. Think about it, which is more exciting? A book about a dad who has to mow the grass and kill a couple of dandelions or . . .

A book about a cute lion cub whose new friend, Charlotte the dandelion, is at risk of being uprooted by Daddy because he's scared of what the neighbors will say?*

Exactly! The second option because the characters are so detailed.

If that's how we describe books when we read them, how much more important should our characters be when we write them? A lot! We want people to describe our lovable characters just as much as the next one.

Consider some picture book characters kids love: *The Pigeon* by Mo Willems, *Pig the Pug* by Aaron Blabey, and *Mother Bruce* by Ryan T. Higgins. What makes these characters household favorites? Their humor, loud personalities, and relatability.

Five important questions about your main character:

Even though you're writing a picture book, that doesn't mean you don't have to know a lot about your character. Remember, the characters need to feel three-dimensional to a reader.

To do this, you must answer the following five basic questions about each character in your book.

✳ · ✳ · ✴ · ✳ · ✳

*Description based on Ame Dyckman's book *Dandy* (Little, Brown, 2019).

1. What is their basic information?

This is probably an automatic question you ask yourself before you start a story. You might think about your main character by listing their name, age, birthday, appearance, etc.

Sometimes, you may develop a basic description quickly, and other times, this requires research. Either way, don't stop there. You must go deeper to build a big personality like the characters previously mentioned. Continue answering the following questions.

2. What's their family dynamic?

Everyone's family is different. As you can imagine, with seven kids growing up in one family, there were many varying personalities. (It's impossible not to with that big of an age gap!)

For instance, my sister is eleven years younger than me. She didn't grow up listening to N'Sync or waiting to have a Facebook account until her junior year of high school, and she didn't have all those house "rules" parents only seem to give the older children. This makes us very different people.

However, whenever there are siblings, although there will be differences, there will also be similarities. For example, I tend to whip out a mother-like personality—and so do all my brothers. (We like to call it pulling a "Joni"—named after our mom.)

And the same is true of your character.

The way a person's family is built can drastically affect how they act in your story. Research birth order traits to know how an older child versus a middle or younger child would act. Know if your character's parents are divorced, and if so, know when it happened. Anything that will help you understand your character better.

3. How are their relationships with people outside of their family?

Along with having a family, your character may also have relationships with lots of other people in the story:

- Teachers
- Friends
- Classmates
- Older kids
- Restaurant & store workers
- Friends' parents, etc.

How do they act when they're around others? Are they the kid who acts out for attention in front of their friends? Are they passive and let their friends make most of the decisions? Does how they act differ depending on who they're with?

We can all change how we act based on who we're around. (Sometimes that's a good thing, sometimes not. Either way, it's a very human thing to do.) The same will be true for your characters, too. And as the writer, you need to know why they change. What underlying factors are playing into their actions at the same time?

Are they trying to be cool or show off? Are they trying to be respectful? Was it how they were raised and the values instilled in them? Keep asking and answering questions to help you get to the deeply rooted answer behind this. Don't stop at surface-level answers.

4. What is their personality like?

I don't know about you, but I LOVE personality quizzes. They always seem to describe me accurately. (Sometimes it makes me wonder if they're part stalker.) But these quizzes aren't just great for killing time on Facebook; they're also excellent for character research.

Do an online search for "personality quizzes for kids" and take a couple as if you're the character in your book. Reading the results will help you build a complete personality. This will help you understand the reasoning behind their selfish or stubborn ways and give you insight into how they might act in certain situations that you can use in your story.

5. What's on their favorites list?

Alongside your character's personality, they're going to have tangible things they like and don't like. For instance, a school subject or school itself, activities they do alone or with friends, favorite movies, books, colors, etc.

But don't just answer them; go deeper. Think about the memories attached to whatever they like or don't like. Why did they decide on that particular item?

It's not enough to just know the quick answers to these questions. You need to understand what influences their decisions in life, their reasons for doing anything, and how they would react in every situation. It's the only way to write a fully developed human versus a two-dimensional stand-in.

What to Do if You Don't Have a Character:

If you're thinking, *Brooke, what if I don't have a character?* Maybe you're writing a nonfiction or concept book, and you have no idea what to do for this section since your idea isn't a character-driven story. Or maybe you're writing a younger picture book and don't have room for a big character.

You still want to make your book fun and memorable, but you might not want to use a specific character to do this. In this situation, I recommend thinking about what point of view you want to tell the story from rather than picking a specific character.

POINT OF VIEW BREAKDOWN

1st	First Person POV: Uses "I/me/my" in the text. Very intimate perspective.
2nd	Second Person POV: Uses "you/your" in the text. Writer speaks directly to the reader.
3rd	Third Person POV: Uses pronouns like "he/him," "she/her," and "they/them." Classic, narrator perspective.

A Breakdown of Point of View:

Point of view (POV) determines the type of character that is right for your book, no matter what kind of story you're telling.

First Person POV: In this point of view, the story uses "I/me/my" in the text. This is an internal, very intimate perspective because the reader knows the character's thoughts, feelings, and motives.

Second Person POV: Here, the reader becomes the character. Using "you/your" in the text, the writer speaks directly to the reader. (Like how I am talking to you in this book.) This is an interactive way to tell a story and works well when you don't have a main character or when writing a concept or nonfiction book.

Third Person POV: This is a classic and very common point of view that uses pronouns like "he/him," "she/her," and "they/them." With this perspective, you talk about a character but don't necessarily reveal all their thoughts and feelings to the reader.

Being aware of the different points of view is crucial. If you aren't sure which POV is right for your character, experiment with different ones to find the best fit for your story. Or rewrite a published picture book from a different point of view and see how that affects the story from the reader's perspective.

A final helpful trick is to think of yourself as a video camera. As the narrator/writer, you need to angle your camera according to the POV you're using.

- In **first person,** the camera is directly through the eyes of the character.

- In **second person,** the camera is pointed directly at the reader.

- In **third person,** the camera is positioned beside the character for the reader to follow along.

When writing your story, always know where your camera sits. This will help you stay grounded in the setting and follow along with your characters, ensuring your reader feels immersed in the story.

It will also prevent you from "head-hopping" or "cheating" when explaining something that happens in your story. Avoid POV hopping for convenience by always considering where your camera is placed.

To help you get started:

- Complete a character profile card. (You can find one inside the workbook at JourneytoKidlit.com/PBP-Free-Resources.)

- Be specific. The more specific you are, the more authentic and real your characters will feel.

- Bring out your character's unique personality in the story.

Once you have your character's unique personality, make sure it's evident throughout the entire story by focusing on three key aspects: action, dialogue, and monologue.

✳ · ✳ · ✳ · ✳ · ✳

1. Action: What your character does.

Your unique character should act according to their personality. If they're an artsy kid, that should be reflected in everything they do. Don't just mention their hobbies or passions; incorporate them into the book.

2. Dialogue: What your character says.

Think about how you can "hear" someone's voice when you read their texts or emails. That's because people often write the way they talk. Even though you're the writer, everything your character says should sound like them. Subtle changes in dialogue can make a big difference, especially in picture books where characters often range in age from 3 to 7. Make sure their speech matches their age.

3. Monologue: What your character thinks.

This is especially important when writing in first person since the narration should sound like your character. If you're using a third-person narrator, make sure the narration fits the target reader's expectations and adds its own voice to the story. No matter what point of view you use, whenever your character is thinking, it should sound authentic to them.

Why all this matters in picture books:

If you're thinking, *This seems like a lot of unnecessary work,* I can assure you it isn't. Besides helping you write an awesome picture book, understanding your character will benefit you in three ways . . .

1. **It elevates your story.**

If your story feels just okay, the problem might be your character. If they can be swapped out with anyone else, they're not a character but a placeholder. You need to tell a real person's story, one that would only be true if it were about them.

2. **A big character can make a common story idea feel fresh.**

Think about retellings of fairy tales or alphabet picture books. The plot might not be new, but a great character can make it feel unique and inventive.

3. **A unique character can help you find a solid idea.**

If you're struggling to find a new idea, focus on creating a unique character. For example, imagine a retelling of *Cinderella*. If your Cinderella is an edgy biker or a wealthy townsperson who has to bail the prince out, you have a fresh take on the story.

Choosing Your Setting

Next, we need to choose the story's setting. I like to think of your book as a peek into your character's "life window." Meaning, they had a life before this story and will have a life after it. Where you choose to peek into their world is what matters.

To create a setting, you need to know the time period and location where the reader meets your character. Where are they in the world?

While your story can take place anywhere you want,

you must establish your world's rules and stick to them. They also must be logical to the reader. For example, if your story takes place in the real world, a dog and a human can't talk to each other. (As much as we wish our pets could talk to us, they can't.)

To create your world's rules, you must know:

- If the setting is magical or not (and how the magic is used if it's included)

- The places your character must go

- The spot where the story _truly_ starts

To help you with the last two bullets, you must know where the reader meets your main character. Are they at home? School? Where are they?

This helps drop your reader into the action and establishes the story goal upfront. Plus, it allows you to quickly introduce the problem—so make sure you know where we're meeting your character.

This brings us to our final ingredient needed for the "gathering your story assets" phase, which will help you know exactly where to start your story.

Determining Your Story Goal or Purpose

Your story goal or focus is the missing piece to make your story feel complete.

To help with this, go back to your character's "life window."

Why is it important for readers to know about this specific moment in your character's life? This gives the reader a reason to care and establishes the point of this story, which will help you pitch and sell your story later.

As you decide your story goal, it's important to understand that there are two types of story goals: Internal and External. Your story should encompass both, but when we're new to writing, we often overlook one or the other. And if you miss the external goal, you don't have a story.

Internal goals:

An internal goal is related to the character's personal growth—hopes, fears, and feelings. It might involve becoming more confident, courageous, kind, strong, or talented.

When I read submissions, I often see internal goals, especially from newer or inexperienced writers.

Internal goals are wonderful because they are about what the character is thinking or feeling. This is where the character's growth comes from and is necessary for their internal arc. But if all you're showing is what they're thinking, imagine a picture book filled with images of brains—that wouldn't work! You need movement in order for a picture book to be engaging for young readers, which is where the external goal comes in.

External goals:

The external goal happens outside of your character and is the driving force of your story—the source of your plot. An external goal can be anything, such as getting rid of a monster in the closet, finding a favorite food, adopting a pet, or going to a friend's birthday party. Since this is a picture book, the external goal doesn't have to be life-altering, but it does have to be there.

To help create a deep connection with your readers, **make your external goal specific.** That's the secret sauce for a great story.

Don't just say, "It's a story about being kind."

Be more specific: "It's a story about a little girl named Sadie who challenges herself to be kind to everyone for 30 days, and what she discovers is life-changing."

Think of external goals like:

- Winning a competition

- Making a friend at school

- Defeating a monster

- Fitting in with the "cool" kids

- Saving the world

Keep in mind that changing your external goal can help you find a better story idea if you're stuck or if you think your idea isn't unique enough.

For example, if you want to write a picture book about moving, there are many ways to approach it:

- A child not wanting to move to a new house

- A friend moving away

- Becoming the new kid at school

The more specific your idea, the better your story will be.

To find your story goal or purpose, ask yourself:

- What does your character want most?

- How can they achieve their inner goal?

- How can the setting help? What might they want from it?

These answers will help you discover their motives and develop your plot.

ACTION STEP:

TO DO!

Complete the Chapter Activity.

Get the Character Profile Card inside the Companion Workbook.

Download it at JourneytoKidlit.com/PBP-Free-Resources if you haven't already.

CHAPTER FOUR

Outlining Your Plot

A S A MEMBER of a large family who grew up surrounded by acres of land but no neighborhood friends, my brothers and I had to find creative ways to entertain ourselves.

This included us drawing elaborate plans for a treehouse that would rival Arthur's and grabbing shovels to try to dig our way through the center of the earth all the way to China. We also pushed several rocks under a weeping willow to form a "club" and stacked them on each other to make houses for frogs we found.

You probably have similar memories of ways you were creative or problems you experienced as a child. Or even problems you've seen your own child go through. This is a great place to form a potential plot outline for your story—so many things can make for a great plot in a children's book.

A plot is a sequence of events that are unveiled throughout a story. But the big thing to note is that your sequence of events must be connected. They are connected through the external goal you established in the "gathering your story assets" section, which is why you do that first. This is your driver—your connector—for all the stuff that happens in terms of your plot.

Three Plot Outlines for Picture Books

In a picture book, you have three plot options to choose from: a classic plot, a midpoint plot, and a list or how-to plot.

PLOT OUTLINES

CLASSIC	Problem/Solution approach. Three Events/Attempts to Climax.
MIDPOINT	Similar to Classic, but includes a "turning point" halfway through the book.
LIST/ HOW-TO	Great for concept books and nonfiction. Includes a list of events or steps to conclusion.

Classic Plot Outline

A classic plot is typically what you think of when asked about a plot. It includes an introduction, followed by the introduction of a problem, with three attempts to try to solve it, and then you reach the end where it's either solved or not solved.

This occurs most commonly in fictional stories, but even

nonfiction and concept books can use a classic plot outline. Choosing the right plot for your story is all about the goal and what will happen as your character tries to achieve said goal.

The classic plot structure step-by-step breakdown:

There are seven components that will make up the classic plot of your picture book. I've laid them out for you below, so all you have to do is plug your idea into this formula every time you write a new story with a classic plot structure. (It's universal and reusable!)

Here are the steps:

Step 1: Introduction

This is the beginning of your story and how you choose to invite the reader into your character's life. How will you do this? Where is your character the moment the reader peeks in?

You'll want to start in one of two ways: introducing us to your character in a fun, entertaining way or dropping us right into the action of a scene. You can learn how to write an awesome introduction by reading lots of new traditionally published picture books. They will help you get a sense of what other writers are doing today.

Step 2: Introduce the Problem

Right after your introduction, let the reader know what problem needs to be solved. This is the primary purpose of your story—the crux of your whole plot. And you should try to let them know the problem within the first 50 words, or first few pages.

How you want to write your problem is up to you, but you need to reveal it quickly, and it needs to be apparent to the reader. (Some writers will even reveal the problem in the first sentence or two.)

Step 3: Solution Attempt #1

Now that we know who the story is about and what problem they need to solve, it's time to find a solution. But we don't want the solution to appear on the very next page—that wouldn't make it a very exciting story.

I recommend using the Rule of Three to have your character try (and fail) three times to solve their problem before they reach the end of the book.

Step 4: Solution Attempt #2

Each time you introduce a new solution attempt, the stakes need to escalate. Unlike a young adult novel with dire stakes, the failures could seem small yet must be relatable and seem big to a young child. For example, your character's friend didn't see the letter he wrote them or everyone still laughed at his hat.

Step 5: Solution Attempt #3

When you make it to the third solution attempt, you want your character and reader to think: *This has to be it, right? We've tried and tried to solve our problem. The solution should be here, right?* But they need to be proven wrong. There's still this last hurdle for your character to overcome.

Step 6: Climax—Sense of Failure or Doubt/Moment of Truth (Did it Work?)

Because your poor character has made three attempts to solve their problem without success, they get a sense that it's never going to work—they're always going to have this problem. They might even be tempted to give up and throw in the towel.

This is what's known in the picture book plot structure as the climax of the book. It's the sense that all hope is lost. Even if it's something as minor as they can't find their favorite food to eat. (To a kid, even the minor stuff is big stuff.)

Make sure you have a sense of this before moving on to the last step.

Step 7: Solution/Ending

Finally! We made it to the ending. Your character finds one more solution that might work to solve their problem . . . and this time it actually does! Now, your character has grown full circle and has turned a new leaf. They've changed from who they were at the start of the book and have found the perfect solution to their problem.

An important thing to note about this final step is that your character MUST solve the problem themselves. They cannot have anyone else, especially a grown-up, do it for them.

Here's an example based on Jannesy DeLeon's book, *Tag! You're It*:

Step 1: Introduction

You meet Gabby being pushed on the swing by her brother. They see some kids playing tag, and Gabby decides she wants to play.

Step 2: Introduce the Problem

Gabby has cerebral palsy and is non-verbal, so she can't run over and join them like any other kid. She needs help.

Step 3: Solution Attempt #1

She gets Nicky's attention so he can push her over to join the other kids. But they don't invite her to join . . . just Nicky.

Step 4: Solution Attempt #2

Gabby gestures that Nicky can push her so she can still play. But the other kids dart around so fast she can't tag any of them.

Step 5: Solution Attempt #3

Gabby has an idea to surprise the kids and tag them when they least expect it. Finally, a girl gets into reach . . .

Step 6: Climax/Sense of Failure or Doubt

Gabby swivels and lunges forward and . . .

Step 7: Solution/Ending

Tags her! Gabby proves to everyone, including herself, that she really can play tag, just like any other kid.

Read the book *Tag! You're It* by Jannesy DeLeon (BiblioKid Publishing, 2022) to see how that looks in real life.

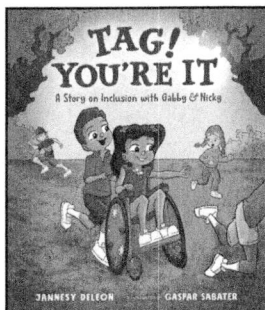

Other books to read with classic plot outlines:

- *Remarkably You* by Pat Zietlow Miller (HarperCollins, 2019)

- *Whobert Whover, Owl Detective* by Jason June (Margaret K. McElderry Books, 2017)

Midpoint Plot Outline

The next outline is the midpoint plot. This is a spinoff from the classic outline. Here, you have an introduction with a problem, but instead of three cut-and-dry attempts to try to solve it, you're going to work your way to a midpoint, and at the midpoint the character will experience what's known as a "turning point."

Maybe they have an updated goal because what they were working toward really wasn't the goal they thought they wanted. Or because of what they've learned so far, they've changed their mind about or approach to get what they want most. And now, they have three new attempts to reach the conclusion.

This is a really great plot outline if you have more of an internal problem but are trying to solve it in an external way.

✦ • ✦ • ✦ • ✦ • ✦

The midpoint plot structure step-by-step breakdown:

Like the Classic Plot Structure, the mid-point plot has seven components. I've laid them out for you below so all you have to do is plug your idea into this formula every time you write a new story with a midpoint plot structure. (It's universal and reusable!)

Here are the steps:

Step 1: Introduction

This is the beginning of your story and how you're choosing to invite the reader into your character's life. How will you do this? Where is your character the moment the reader peeks in?

Step 2: Introduce the Problem

Right after your introduction, you must let the reader know what problem needs to be solved. Then catalyze them into finding a solution.

Step 3: Solution Attempt #1
(Occurs with Three Steps)

Now that we know who the story is about and what problem we need to solve, it's time to find a solution. Instead of only having three separate attempts, with this plot structure, you will use the Rule of Three to help your character attempt to solve their problem with their first strategy. Or you'll use it to help them prepare for what's to come at the midpoint.

For example, in *Mother Bruce* by Ryan T. Higgins (Disney Hyperion, 2015), the character wants to get rid of the new goslings that hatched, so he tries three ways to get them to leave. But in *High Five* by Adam Rubin (Dial Books, 2019), the character must first prepare for a high five competition in the first half of the book before getting to the midpoint, which is the start of the competition.

Step 4: Reach Midpoint and Complete a Turning Event

The midpoint is then when the change occurs. Either the character fails and must choose a new path forward, as Bruce did, or they must move into the next phase, as the character in *High Five* did. The turning point could also be a change of heart due to their experience from the three previous attempts. The key here is for your character to make a change, typically a 180-degree turn from where they were going to the next phase.

Step 5: Solution Attempt #2
(Three Attempts to Complete It)

Once they've determined the new course of action, the character will then use three more attempts to achieve their new goal, whatever that is, but each of those three things should still build on each other to lead toward a climax.

Step 6: Climax

This is the moment of ultimate truth about whether they will succeed in the end.

Step 7: Solution/Ending

Which leads us to how it ends. No matter what, your character needs to have reached the solution through their own decision-making, even if they had a guide to help them along the way.

Here's an example based on my book, *This is My Castle:*

Step 1: Introduction

Regan wants to play in the castle.

Step 2: Introduce the Problem

But her sister has a friend over and won't let her join. So Regan must go in search of her own castle.

Step 3: Solution Attempt #1
(Occurs with Three Steps)

She tries the garden shed and to catch a frog to turn him into a prince, but neither will make a good castle. That's when she sees the best castle ever!

Step 4: Reach Midpoint and Complete a Turning Event

Except there's already someone there. Now, she must find a way to get him to leave so she can have the castle all to herself.

Step 5: Solution Attempt #2
(Three Attempts to Complete It)

She tries negotiating with him for the other "castles," but he won't move. Finally, they race to see who gets to stay, and Regan wins.

Step 6: Climax

The boy leaves, and Regan realizes it's lonely being in a castle with no one to play with. So . . .

Step 7: Solution/Ending

She invites him back to play princesses in her castle.

Read the book *This is My Castle* by Brooke Van Sickle (BiblioKid Publishing, 2020) to see how that looks in real life.

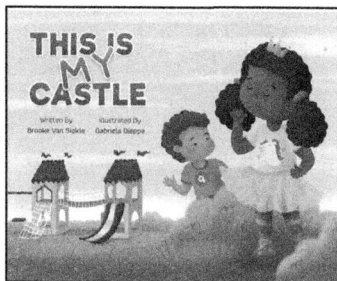

Other books to read with midpoint plot outlines:

- *Mother Bruce* by Ryan T. Higgins (Disney Hyperion, 2015)

- *High Five* by Adam Rubin (Dial Books, 2019)

List or How-to Plot Outline

The last plot option is what's known as a list plot or how-to plot. This is a really great option for STEM, nonfiction, and concept books.

The list or how-to plot structure step-by-step breakdown:

Unlike the other plot outlines, this one has fewer steps because most of the content will occur within the list itself.

Here are the steps:

Step 1: Introduction

For this plot outline, we introduce the goal with the problem, just like we would with all our other ones, except we're going to take a bunch of steps to accomplish it. You want to be sure to include this section so the reader is grounded in your story goal.

It's also good to use a transitional sentence to guide the reader into the list. That way, it feels like you're taking them on a journey rather than dropping them into a random list of information without any facts. For instance, in my book *Pirates Stuck at "C,"* I used the line "Crossbones peered from the crow's nest. Then the captain started his search." to signal my catalyst for the reader into the story.

Step 2: The Steps to Reach the Solution

Sometimes the number of steps is already set for you. Like in an alphabet book, you know it's going to have twenty-six steps because there are 26 letters in the alphabet. However, if it's not predetermined, you may need to pick the number yourself.

On average, most list plots include five to seven steps if the number isn't predetermined. When deciding, make sure to choose a number that won't slow the pace, take too long to get to a conclusion, or wrap the story up too quickly. You should be able to determine if it feels too long and where you can possibly start cutting, or if it doesn't feel like you've done enough, after you've read through your first draft.

Step 3: Solution/Ending

After you've completed the number of steps needed to complete the list, wrap it all up with an ending or final line to make the story feel complete.

Here's an example based on my book, *Pirates Stuck at "C"*:

Step 1: Introduction

Captain Scallywag and his crew sail to an island for treasure. They drop the anchor and begin their search.

Step 2: The Steps to Complete the Solution

Each pirate and the corresponding letter have an action that leads them closer to the treasure—seemingly to no avail—until Vladimir shouts, "Victory, Captain!"

Step 3: Solution/Ending

Captain Scallywag and Wally wade through the water and find their treasure. The crew board the ship and sail away after a successful day of treasure hunting.

Read the book *Pirates Stuck at "C"* by Brooke Van Sickle (BiblioKid Publishing, 2020) to see how that looks in real life.

Other books to read with list or how to plot outlines:

- *B is for Bananas* by Carrie Tillotson (Flamingo Books, 2023)
- *The Very Impatient Caterpillar* by Ross Burach (Scholastic, 2019)

Making Characters and Plot Work Together

Now that you understand how to build a strong character for your picture book and have a basic understanding of the plot, it's time to mold them together. Remember we talked about your character and how all their decisions and all their reactions will drive your plot and move the story along.

Here are four ways your character's unique personality will directly affect your plot:

1. Through the internal story arc.

In every picture book, your character must go through a stage of growth. By the time we reach the end, your character should change slightly from who they were at the beginning or learn something new. This is known as your internal character arc.

2. Your character's reaction determines what happens next.

As humans, we know we can't always control what happens in our lives, but we can choose how we react. And the same is true for you as the writer of your character.

As you're thinking about the events or attempts that will occur in your plot outline, make sure to choose the most authentic reaction your character would have to the situation that you've laid in front of them. Think "this, then this, then this" as the connector to move from scene to scene.

3. The main character must be active.

Because picture books are very visual, you want your characters to constantly move. This means your story cannot consist of a bunch of action that happens with you telling us about each of these things. Instead, go back to the visual with the video camera and your character to ensure you're moving with them throughout the story as the reader.

4. They must solve the problem.

This is especially important in picture books to teach independence and problem-solving, but it will also help you develop the unique twist or ending that will make your story stand out to a reader. If you're thinking about how your character will respond to the situations you've thrown at them, then you can naturally decide how they will try to solve them, too.

Using the rule of three:

I mentioned the "Rule of Three" earlier, so I wanted to make sure to give you more information about it and how to use it to your advantage because it's a pretty great tool to use in picture books. This rule can help you with the rhythm and pacing of your story, page turns, and help you make sure you have enough action in your story before reaching the end.

You can use the Rule of Three either in forms of:

- Repetition—by repeating the same word three times or by using a series of three words to describe a noise or action. For example: clink, clank, clunk.

- **Through the action itself**—listing three different things a character did instead of just saying this happened. For example, they washed, dried, and folded the laundry instead of saying they did the laundry.

- By listing three separate attempts at something—
which is how we used it in the plot outlines.

Let's look at each of those in action using my own picture books.

Repetition using the rule of three:

Repetition is one of my favorite ways to use the Rule of Three and add flavor to your picture book because it adds an element of fun and play without changing your story. I also love that it allows for alliteration and a combination of similar sounds, which leads to great read-aloud appeal for all readers. Plus, kids enjoy when they get to help read by repeating a word.

For example, *This is My Castle* describes what's happening as Regan tries to find a castle to play in. In the scene we're going to look at, the main character has recently spotted a frog hopping by and has the idea that if she catches him, she can kiss him to turn him into a prince and steal his castle.

Here's how that reads in the story using the Rule of Three:

This is NOT my castle. I will have to find another.

(Illustrator Note: Regan sees a toad hopping by.)

Hop,
Hop,
Hop.
"STOP TOAD!" I shout.
If I catch him, I can turn him
into a prince with a kiss.
Then take his castle.

(Illustrator Note: Regan runs after the toad but it escapes into the pond.)

Huff,
Huff,
Huff.
That toad sure is speedy!
He will NOT help me get my castle. I will have to find
another.

Do you see the repetition with the Rule of Three to show the toad hopping by? And then again, to show how exhausted Regan is from running after him? As you can see, adding these repetitive words didn't change the story or the plot; it just elevated it and made it more enjoyable for young readers.

Action using the rule of three:

When you're trying to say someone did something in a picture book, it's better to break it down into smaller steps. So, instead of saying they went to school, you could say how they got there by skipping across the street, ducking past the neighbor's house, and waving to the crossing guard. (Or something that adds humor and entertainment to your story.)

As a picture book writer, you must choose your words wisely—remember, picture books should be less than 600 words. So, you shouldn't describe how things look and use descriptive words like you would in a novel. (That's what the illustrations are for!) However, you have freedom to play with your words and approach the action from an element of enjoyment for the reader.

Let's look at an excerpt from *Humans In-Training* (BiblioKid Publishing, 2020) as an example. In the following scene, the main character, Kobe, has recently been adopted and is disappointed with how his new dog parents behave. So he's decided that he's going to have to train them in order to get what he wants.

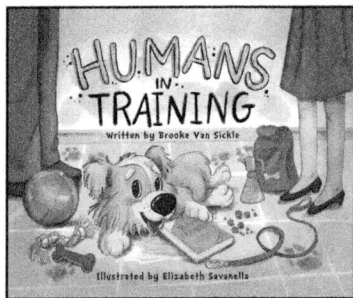

Here's how that reads in the story using the Rule of Three:

> *I thought I'd be living in the lap of luxury when*
> *I first moved in.*
> *There was everything a dog could need.*
>   *Fenced in yard,*
>   *Food dish in sight,*
>   *and . . . PLENTY of space to spread out.*
>   *But I soon realized my humans*
>   *had a lot to learn.*
> *At first, my humans slept like cats*
> *and were as selfish as squirrels.*
>   *They were as exciting as a chewed-up toy.*
>   *If I wanted to live the dog's life, I needed to train my*
>   *humans.*

Do you see how the action was used with the Rule of Three to show what Kobe's life is like—with a yard, food dish, and plenty of space—and the three things his humans did to upset him as clarified through the illustrations? They slept in (like cats), were as selfish as squirrels (didn't share their food with him), and were as exciting as a chewed-up toy (ignored him or were on their phones). All things that, from a dog's perspective, would be quite annoying.

Page-turns using the rule of three:

The final example we're going to look at for the Rule of Three is through different attempts, which can be elevated in picture books through page turns. This not only helps to keep the story moving, but it can also help remind the reader of the story's purpose—or the plot—as they read.

Let's look at an excerpt from *Pirates Stuck at "C"* as an example.

> Back on land, Gus dragged the gangplank and Harry captured the horizon.
>
> **But none of the pirates found any treasure.**
>
> Igor licked an ice cream cone and Jughead jumped from a jellyfish sting.
>
> Killian was tangled in kelp and Larry had a lobster clamped to his toe.
>
> **But none of the pirates found any treasure.**
>
> Captain Scallywag traveled deeper into the island and found . . .
>
> Marty splashing with mermaids and Ned taking his afternoon nap.
> Ollie was the only pirate not enjoying the lagoon.

Paulie experimented with plankton.
and Quinn wrote notes with her quill.
But none of the pirates found any treasure.

With this story, the phrase "but none of the pirates found any treasure" was used to keep the story moving along and remind the reader they're supposed to be looking for treasure as they read. This is also something that kids enjoy repeating as the story is being read to them.

Before you move on, make sure to solidify your assets and think through your plot outline. I'll see you in the next chapter to begin writing your first draft!

ACTION STEP:

Complete the Chapter Activity.

Get the Story Plot Checklist
inside the Companion Workbook.

Download it at JourneytoKidlit.com/PBP-Free-
Resources if you haven't already.

TO DO!

CHAPTER FIVE

Writing Your Picture Book

I'VE ALWAYS BEEN a big reader, but after I became a mom, I wanted to make reading a pastime my son and I did together. We've read so many board books and picture books over the years—some great and some not so great.

As I read though, I often find myself thinking, *I'd love to publish a book like this.* Or, *Wow, this gives me an idea for my own children's book that I could write.*

What about you? Have you ever looked at a children's book and thought this is something you might be able to do, too?

Maybe that's why you began this journey and purchased this book. Maybe you never expected to be a writer, and now you're really intimidated over the idea of writing something that kids will love and feel connected to.

I get it.

Whether this is your first book or you've been writing for a long time without any publishing success, the pressure to create something amazing can weigh on you. But I want you to know that you can do this! You don't need a writing degree or need to be a master writer to write the book of your dreams. You just need to tell an engaging story that kids and parents will enjoy, which is what I'm going to help you do.

Writing a picture book is a combination of things that all work together to tell a great story, including the text itself, illustrations, and read-out-loud appeal. This is unique compared with all other kinds of writing because, for the most part, your target reader will not be reading the book themselves.

Instead, this is an interactive type of reading where you will want to appease both adults and children. Whether you're aiming for a traditional publishing contract or self-publishing, this matters because your reader is your audience. And if you can't earn their trust with a well-told story, it'll be hard to engage them for future books.

Three key ingredients you need for a successful picture book:

1. A Solid Story

You need a well-crafted story. The editors at a publishing house can't spend endless hours fixing your plot, so you need strong story elements in place before submitting to them. This includes everything we chatted about in the previous two chapters. As you write your first draft, be sure to review whether you have a complete story or just bits and pieces.

Make sure you introduce your readers to your setting, main character, and story goal within the first 50 to 80 words so they quickly know why they should care about the story—why it matters and why they should keep reading.

2. High Readability

The story must be something people enjoy reading and want to share. The goal should be to have your readers feel connected to the characters, understand their goals, and feel compelled to keep reading.

The reader needs to understand what's happening and feel immersed in the world you've created. Strong word choice is imperative no matter if you're using verbs, sounds, smells, emotions—whatever. Every word must serve a purpose because you have so few you can use. Use the right words to show what's happening, and make sure your character's personality shines through their actions.

3. Great Marketability

As much as we love our stories, they are products. Can you sell it? Is there an audience for it? You need to ensure your story has potential in the market.

If you plan on getting this book published, you need to know how to market your book. Even though you might not handle all the marketing yourself, you should understand how to pitch it. Comp books (comparable books) will help show that there's a market for your story, but it's your job as you write your book to create something that will stand out next to the competition.

Before you begin writing, please note this:

If you're like me and struggle with perfectionism, please know that this first draft is expected to be crappy. It doesn't have to be perfect because you will get to edit it.

I had to quickly learn this—whenever I would begin a new draft, I'd clam up and feel too much pressure to write something amazing. This used to prevent me from writing anything for a long time. (Which doesn't exactly work when you're trying to be a full-time children's book author.)

To overcome my perfectionism, I learned how to become a great editor and write a crummy first draft in order to move forward. This might be something you have to do, too. And that's okay! Remember, all writing is good writing because it's helping you become a better writer.

Over the remainder of this chapter and the next chapter, I will help guide you on how to write a good story. But first, let's talk about formatting.

What Does a Picture Book Manuscript Look Like?

When you think of a picture book, you probably think of the finished product—a 32-page book with illustrations and a cover. But that's not how picture books start out, especially if you're the author only, and not an author-illustrator.

In the previous chapter, I gave you a brief look at how a picture book looks as a manuscript with the examples from my own stories. However, I want to give you a full breakdown here as well.

(There's also a sample manuscript inside the companion workbook. If you haven't gotten it yet, download it at JourneytoKidlit.com/PBP-Free-Resources.)

Here's what your manuscript should look like:

Unlike what most people think, a picture book manuscript should be created as a standard Word document that's double-spaced, using Times New Roman, 12-point font. It'll be written following the paragraph formatting you learned in school, instead of 32 separate pages for each page break you envision. (Most picture book manuscripts don't exceed four or five typed pages.)

MANUSCRIPT EXAMPLE

Van Sickle/Amazing Title 1

Brooke Van Sickle
Address
City, State Zip
Phone
Email

Picture Book age 4-7
About 350 words

MY CURIOSITY INVOKING TITLE
By: Brooke Van Sickle

I indent the great first line of my story.

Set up with double-spacing.

And when I say something that requires an illustrator note.

Illustrator Note: I put it here

Then I keep going with my story.

Until I reach the end. (Remember - picture books should be about 500-600 words at most and should leave anything descriptive to the illustrator.)

To help you set up your manuscript correctly, here are the six important things to note about your manuscript:

1. **Contact Information and Book Category**—In the upper, left-hand corner of your Word document, include your contact information. Then tab over to the right side and type your category and age range. The next line (where you've listed your address) should also include your word count. This way your contact and book information are on the same line.

2. **Title and Byline**—This will be centered about halfway down the page. Your title should be written in ALL CAPS with the byline, or "written by" line, directly underneath. (You can also slide a sub-header between the two if needed.)

3. **Sentence Structure**—If you write in short, snappy sentences, there's no need to indent. However, if you have more than one sentence per stanza, be sure to indent the first line like you would any new paragraph.

4. **Illustrator Notes**—We will cover these in a later chapter, but you may want to include them as needed in your manuscript. To add an illustrator note, add a new line aligned to the right and choose a different font size, color, or italicize to differentiate it from the rest of the manuscript. This way, the reader won't really notice them as they read.

5. **Punctuation**—Unlike a novel, where you're writing full paragraphs, a picture book manuscript can be more free-flowing to allow for rhythm and page turns. This means that not every line has to be a full or complete sentence. You can break them up as you go down the page. (Just be

sure to use proper spelling and grammar like you would in any other document.)

6. **Page Numbers**—Type your first name and last name in the header of your manuscript, followed by the page number. This should be included on every page in the right corner.

It's a good habit to start formatting your stories correctly every time you start a new draft so it's ready when you submit for either a critique or publication. If this is your first time writing a children's book, the number one exercise I recommend is to type out recently published books as manuscripts as though you were the author of them.

This will not only show you what the book looks like without illustrations, but it'll give you an example of picture book voice, sentence structure, and story length that you'll want to aim for as you're writing your own story. I have a folder called "Picture Book Practice" saved to my Google Drive that's filled with example manuscripts of published picture books. And it's been hands-down the best teaching tool for me as a writer. I highly recommend you try it.

Elements to Incorporate in Your Writing

Alongside the Rule of Three, there is a rhythm to picture books you'll want to incorporate. This is obvious to hear when you're creating or reading a rhyming book, but even when it doesn't rhyme, there's still a rhythm.

If you're well-versed in poetry or have a knowledge of

writing music, it might be easier for you to hear and write with a rhythm in mind. However, if you're like me and are not a poet by any means, there are some alternative rhythms outside of a rhyming pattern that you can use to help you write.

- As you read, try clapping along to hear how the syllables and words read together. Does it stick to a beat?

- There should be a variety in the word sounds as you read. Do you notice your voice rising and falling? Do you ever end on a sentence where it sounds flat or dull?

- Are there any similar-sounding words you can add that incorporate a sense of rhythm without having to make it rhyme?

ELEMENTS TO IMPROVE WRITING

1	Onomatopoeia: Using a word that phonetically imitates, resembles, or suggests a sound.
2	Simile: Describing something like or as something else.
3	Metaphor: Referring to something as something else entirely.
4	Personification: Giving human traits to a non-human object.

You can see how this is done well by reading previously published picture books and noticing how the authors write their stories. One of my favorite writers to do this with is Tammi Sauer. (She also writes hilarious and well-thought-out stories, so she's just a good author to study in general.) To get started, check out *The Underpants* (Scholastic, 2023) or *Mary Had a Little Plan* (Union Square, 2022).

If you're a writer who'd like to write rhyming picture books, Josh Funk is a master in spinning rhymes that children love. His book *Lady Pancake & Sir French Toast* (Scholastic, 2015) was such a big hit that there have been multiple spin-off successes. For more recent rhyming picture books, read books by Pat Zietlow Miller or books like *I Will Read to You* by Gideon Steer (Little Brown, 2023) to get a better feel for more recently published rhyming picture books.

> **NOTE:** Picture books do NOT have to rhyme. And if you're going to rhyme, it has to be a true rhyme, which is a lot harder than it seems. If your story feels forced or the rhyme is preventing you from being creative and telling the story in a way that will do it justice, try removing the rhyme from your writing.

Now that you've got a handle on the Rule of Three and rhythm for your story, you can start to get creative with your word or phrase choices in your story. When you use certain elements in your manuscript, it will make it so much more fun to read and write.

Try Figurative language like:

- **Onomatopoeia**—Using a word that phonetically imitates, resembles, or suggests a sound is being heard. Like "Bang," "Meow," "Crinkle."

- **Simile**—Describing something like or as something else. For example, he is as brazen as an ox.

- **Metaphor**—Referring to something as something else entirely. For example, my sister is the shrimp of the family. (She's not actually a shrimp. She's just shorter than everyone else.)

- **Personification**—Giving human traits to a non-human object. Like Pixar does in movies such as *Cars* (2006) and *Ratatouille* (2007).

These elements can help you really get creative and find the uniqueness in your story idea. For instance, if you're trying to do a re-telling of *Cinderella*, maybe you choose to tell it from the mice's perspective and give them human traits or even pretend as if they're Cinderella. That would be personification at work.

Using Dialogue in Your Story

Dialogue is a key part of our stories but also something that many writers get wrong.

What characters say, how they say it, and when they talk all matter. This is especially true in chapter books and novels, but it's also important in picture books. We'll talk about why in a bit, but first, let's break down what makes up a story.

A story usually has three main parts: action, description, and dialogue. When you're writing a story, you need to include all three. In picture books, most descriptions come from the illustrations, so there will likely be a lot more of both action and dialogue, but it's important to have a good balance to tell a full story.

How to Add Dialogue:

Dialogue in your story should feel like a conversation. It can be between two characters or a character talking to themselves, known as internal dialogue. However, especially in picture books, we don't want our characters to be still for too long or in their heads too much—we need to see things happening. It's important to think more outwardly than inwardly for everything in a picture book, even for dialogue.

Here are three best practices for using dialogue in your story:

1. To Move the Story Forward

When you add dialogue, it should always move the story forward. If the dialogue doesn't move the story forward, it can slow the pace and make it feel like the characters aren't doing anything. You should try to avoid having your characters stand in one spot, talking back and forth for too long. Otherwise, it will be a similar illustration page after page, which won't be fun for anyone to read.

2. To Add Character Personalization

Dialogue also shows the personality of your characters. The way characters speak should reflect who they are. For example, when someone texts you using someone else's number, you can typically tell because it doesn't sound quite like them. It's the same with your characters. Each character should have their own way of speaking. They shouldn't all sound the same. This doesn't mean you must add accents or catchphrases unless they fit the character. Instead, simply focus on how your character would naturally talk based on who they are.

3. To Reveal Important Information

Dialogue is also a good way to give information, but be careful not to overload the reader with information. This can slow down the pacing and make the story boring. In picture books, it's especially important to avoid long dialogue scenes without any action or movement. Otherwise, the story doesn't move forward, and the plot doesn't develop.

Here's an example of how I used dialogue in *This Is My Castle*. In this scene, Regan has found a castle to play in, but there's already a boy there.

> "INVADER!" *I shout.*
>
> *This is NOT his castle. He will have to find another.*
>
> *I puff up my chest and wave my hand like I own the place* ('*Cause I do*). "*You may leave now,*" *I say and shoo him away.*
>
> *But the boy doesn't move.*
>
> *He must leave. This is MY castle!*
>
> *I have an idea. He can have the gnome castle.*
>
> "*Oh no, not gnomes. My big brother says gnomes eat your toes!*" *he says.*

Okay . . . He can have the toad's castle!

"Oh no, not toads. My big brother says toads give you warts!" he says.

"Then go play with your big brother!" I shout.

"My big brother never wants to play with me . . ." he says.

I know all about people not wanting to play with you.

See how the dialogue is used to show a bit of the characters' personalities and add emotion without slowing the story's pace? That's how you want to use dialogue in your story, too.

Choosing Your Story Title

The final thing to consider as you write your manuscript is your book's title. The title of your book is really important because it's the first thing a reader sees. Like a first impression, it grabs the reader's attention and makes them want to know more about your story. But picking a title can be tough. It might seem like a lot of pressure since you must choose only a few words to represent your whole story.

How do you choose the right title? And how do you know if it's catchy enough or coming from the right point of view?

The Purpose of Your Title:

The title's job is to tell the reader what your story is about in just a few words. It also needs to spark their curiosity—like a hook that makes them say, "Ooh, tell me more!" Your title should make someone want to open the book and start reading.

Imagine walking down the aisles of Barnes and Noble and looking at all the books. A fun title might make you pick up a book to see what it's about. That's what your title needs to do, too.

How to Pick a Good Title:

Titles are something we talk about a lot in Kidlit Academy because, as an editor and publisher, I often see titles that don't quite match the story or ones that are too generic to hook a reader. How can you avoid that and choose a title that's just right?

There are three main places to look for a good title idea for your story:

1. The Character's Name

Sometimes, using the main character's name as the title works well, especially if the character is unique or has a standout personality. For example, *Mother Bruce* by Ryan T. Higgins (Disney Hyperion, 2015) or *The Adventures of Beekle: The Unimaginary Friend* by Dan Santat (Little, Brown, 2015) are titles where the main character's name is the focus.

2. The Main Goal or Problem

Another option is to use the story's main goal or problem in the title. This type of title gives readers a hint about what the story is about. For example, *The Girl Who Could Fix Anything: Beatrice Shilling, World War II Engineer* by Mara Rockliff (Candlewick, 2021) or *The Day The Crayons Quit* by Drew Daywalt (Philomel, 2013) are titles that tell you right away what the main challenge or goal of the story is.

3. The Main Theme or Takeaway

If your story has a strong theme or lesson, you can use that in your title. For example, *The Wonderful Things You Will Be* by Emily Winfield Martin (Puffin, 2020) lets the reader know from the title that this is a book about who your child might become as they grow up. And *When You Are Brave* by Pat Zietlow Miller (Little, Brown, 2019) is clear from the title that it will be about courage or bravery.

How to find the perfect title for your story:

1. **Write Your Story Pitch:** Start by writing a one-sentence pitch for your story. This helps you focus on the main character, the problem, and the goal. (I have a pitch formula you can use in Chapter Nine to help you get started.)

2. **Pull Key Phrases from Your Story:** Look for important lines, phrases, or ideas in your story that stand out and capture the essence of your book.

3. **Brainstorm a List of Titles:** Make a list of ten to twenty possible titles. The first one you think of might not be the best, but as you keep brainstorming, you'll start to find the one that fits just right.

Remember, your title is the first thing readers see, so take your time and choose one that really captures what your story is all about. And before you move forward with a title, do an online search to see if there are other books with the same or similar title. If there are too many books with the same title as yours, then readers might have a difficult time finding your specific book. Plus, having a unique title helps with the marketability for your book.

———◦◦◇◦◦———

You're ready to start writing your first draft, so dive in! (Remember, it doesn't have to be perfect—in fact, it shouldn't be.) Try not to edit as you write; this helps the story flow naturally.

If you get stuck or your word count feels too high, keep going until you reach the end. Even if the story poured out of you in the middle of the night, this is just the first version. We'll refine it together.

You can revisit the suggestions above to edit your draft, or when you're ready, move on to the next chapter to learn how to officially begin the editing process.

ACTION STEP:

TO DO!

ACTIVITY #3 - SETTING UP YOUR PICTURE BOOK

Complete the Chapter Activity.

Get the Story Set Up
activity inside the Companion Workbook.

Download it at JourneytoKidlit.com/PBP-Free-Resources if you haven't already.

CHAPTER SIX

Editing Your Picture Book

EDITING IS PROBABLY my favorite part of the writing process. As I said in the previous chapter, I really struggle when writing a first draft, but I can easily edit words once I have them on a page.

My goal is to help you feel confident editing your story and to also teach you that your first draft is NOT your best draft. You will ALWAYS need to edit it. Even if you woke up with an amazing idea that just came to you, I promise, the story will be better with at least three more editing rounds. (If not more.)

The Four Types of Story Edits

Before we dive into how to edit your story, you need to know the different kinds of edits your story will need. This is especially important if you ever consider hiring an editor. It will show you the order in which edits are typically conducted in.

As a publisher, I read so many manuscripts that have been "edited" yet aren't actually publishing-ready. I don't want you to make that same mistake, so below are the four main types of edits your story should go through.

TYPES OF STORY EDITS

1	Developmental Edit: First place to start when you edit. Covers "big picture" items.
2	Line Edit: Going line-by-line through your story to ensure that it makes sense and incorporates your story voice and intentions.
3	Copy Edit: Edit to evaluate the manuscript for length, sentence structure, and consistency.
4	Final Proof: Check for any spelling, grammar, and punctuation errors before it's considered publishing-ready.

1. Developmental Edit

The first place you need to start when you edit your story is with the big-picture items. In the editing world, this is known as a developmental edit, and it looks at your plot, characters, and how well they were implemented.

This is also a good time to check that you've included the three things we discussed in Chapter Three, as well as review your story's marketability. Is it clear whose story this is, what it's about, and why the reader should care? If not, this is what you need to edit first.

> **NOTE:** Most professional critiques will give you a high-level developmental edit. (This means it won't be as in-depth as a true developmental edit, but it's a good

place to start.) If you have a strong writing community or peer critique group, they can also help provide you with similar feedback.

2. Line Edit

Once you know all your big-picture items are in place, the next step is to line edit your story. An editor might use this term differently, but in terms of your story, I want you to think about line editing as the way to evaluate your story line-by line.

When conducting a line edit, you'll want to evaluate your manuscript to ensure that it makes sense, that the characters feel authentic, and to find places to add more story voice. During this editing round, I normally like adding "fun" factors or playing with theme-related phrasing.

In the following sections of this chapter, I'll give you ideas on how to do this.

3. Copy Edit

The next edit is the one that many people first think about when they think of "editing." However, as you can see, it comes much later in the process. This is where you need to evaluate the manuscript for length, sentence structure, and consistency. For example, if you say they flipped a coin on page ten and it is tails up, it needs to stay tails up on page twelve.

During this editing round, I like to try to come up with a solid title idea, because, by this point, you should have a clear understanding of what your story is about. I also like to "paginate" my story during this editing stage.

Paginating means thinking about where the text would fall in terms of the 32-page layout.

NOTE: The workbook includes the Picture Book Page Layout Template. Get it for free at JourneytoKidlit.com/ PBP-Free-Resources if you haven't already.

If you've been doing your homework and typing out published picture books, you'll notice they're not all fully illustrated, two-page spreads. There can also be multiple images on a page, so play with your pagination as much as you do your text formatting. Also, use this time to make sure your story isn't too long for a standard picture book length.

4. Final Proof

Finally, the last type of edit you'll want to do is a final proof. This is when you'll check your story for spelling, grammar, and punctuation errors before it's considered publishing-ready.

I always recommend working through these four edits as "rounds" with your manuscript. This means you should have at least four to five drafts of your story before considering it finished. And you might have more. (I wrote 30 different drafts of *Pirates Stuck at "C"* before it was published.)

If you're considering hiring an editor for your book, make sure to start with a developmental edit and try to work with the same editor or editing team. That way, you have a consistent flow with your story. (And make sure they understand how to write and edit a children's book. Not all editors will be able to edit a picture book because the writing style is different compared to writing chapter books or novels.)

Now, if the idea of editing intimidates you or you don't feel qualified to edit your story, I want you to know that's okay. I have four easy tricks to help you get started.

Four Easy Editing Tricks to Use with Every Story

While it's always important to make sure you have all the big picture items in place—like your character, setting, and story goal—before you begin line editing, it can sometimes feel intimidating to try to cut words from your manuscript or write it in a way that appeals to kids. I don't want you to feel stuck looking at your story, so here are four of the easiest ways to edit your manuscript that will increase reader enjoyment and overall readability.

1. Vary your verb choice.

What you use for a verb can make a big difference in your story. For instance, if Sam skipped to school, you might assume he is happy or excited. However, if you say Sam stomped to school, you might assume he is angry or that something is wrong.

We didn't do anything new with the sentence other than change the verb, but that slight swap made a HUGE change to the character's emotion. This is important to do for a couple of different reasons.

One, you want to use a variety of words because picture books are so short. No one wants to read: *Cheryl ran to the market. Cheryl walked to school. Cheryl ran back home.* It's boring. Swap it up.

PRO TIP: I try not to repeat any verbs in my manuscript if I can help it.

And two, your verb choice controls the tone and action of your character. This is a good time to have critique partners because you might not know you used a confusing word. For instance, I like to say someone "screeched to a halt," but readers may get confused about how a human can physically do that since that phrase normally only applies to cars. Make sure the verb you've chosen makes sense to the story and that you're using it correctly.

> ACTION: Highlight all the verbs in your manuscript. If you've repeated any, change them out for a better choice. Then try to replace any other verbs to add emotions or descriptive detail without adding more words or using a word that doesn't quite fit. (Use the thesaurus to find synonyms as needed.)

2. Change any word that ends in "-ing" or "-ly" to an active verb.

A common phrase writing coaches use is "show, don't tell." This means that everything you write should show the reader what's happening in the story without being a list of everything that has already happened. I've found the best way to do this is by looking for any words that end in "-ing" or "-ly."

For example, "Gerald was racing up the stairs" reads as though you're getting information after the fact. If I wanted to show you that, I would instead write, "Gerald raced up the stairs." That puts you in the same room with the character.

Another example would be "Sarah skipped to school" rather than "Sarah happily walked to school." This shows how she feels rather than tells us.

ACTION: Hit Ctrl + F (or Command + F if you are using a Mac) to search your manuscript for any '-ing' or '-ly' words you've used to describe what's happening. If you find any, you should delete them and replace them with something more active.

3. Remove unnecessary description.

When your audience is kids with short attention spans, what you spend your time telling them matters. Especially in picture books.

Since picture books will have illustrations to accompany the words, you want to avoid being too descriptive. This means you shouldn't add in many descriptive lines like "tears streamed down her face" or "he wore a bright blue backpack to school." Those are things the illustrations will show. (You can always add an illustrator note here if you think they won't show it.)

ACTION: Read through your manuscript and remove any unnecessary descriptions or anything that describes what something looks like. Remember, picture books shouldn't be any more than 500–600 words, so this will be really helpful to get you to trim your word count, too.

4. Read your story out loud.

I do this with everything I write—picture books, emails, even this book. Sometimes, what I think makes sense in my head makes zero sense when I try to read it out loud. Instead, I stumble like I'm running on gravel. (Not something you'd want to read!) You also need to do this with your own writing.

It will help you hear the rhythm we talked about earlier

and know how your story will sound when it's read aloud by a first-time reader. This is especially important since a picture book will be read aloud almost every time.

> ACTION: Read your draft out loud to yourself and note where you stumble. (If you want to go a step further, record yourself reading and play it back, or have a friend read it to you.) Whenever you trip up or hear a phrase that sounds awkward, tweak the text until it reads correctly.

Advanced Writing Tips to Improve Your Story

Before we move to the next chapter, I want to also mention some advanced writing techniques that can improve your writing and help you craft a better story. These tips will help you find your voice, make the most of your sentences, and use punctuation and other tools to your advantage.

Things to Play with in Your Writing:

- Theme-specific phrasing
- Punctuation to signal a page-turn
- Formatting to add story voice

Let's take a look at some examples using my stories again, starting with an excerpt from *Pirates Stuck at "C."* For this story, I wanted to explain the process of how pirates might look for treasure while playing with "piratey" words based on each letter in the alphabet.

Captain Scallywag **sailed** *his ship onto the shore.*

It was the perfect place for a treasure hunt.

Arnold **dropped the anchor** *to hold the ship in place*

while Barry sent **messages in a bottle.**

Crossbones peered from the **crow's nest.**

Then the captain started his search.

Captain Scallywag dove into the sea and found . . .

Darryl in deep waters.

While Eric chased an eel

and Frank swam with fish.

Back on land, Gus dragged the **gangplank**

and Harry captured the horizon.

But none of the pirates found any treasure.

Do you see how the story takes the reader on an adventure as though you're right with the pirates? This is a great way to show the reader what's happening and help you feel grounded in the story.

Also, note the use of ellipses after the word found. This is how to incorporate a "page turn" and help build reader anticipation in your book. You can also use an em dash (—) to signal a page turn.

Let's take a look at another example. This time from *This Is My Castle*.

For this book, I wanted to create a story about a little girl whose older sister doesn't want to play with her when she has a friend over. (If you've ever been a younger sibling, I'm sure you can relate to this.) While this story is about sharing and being kind to others, I wanted to give it an imaginative and fun element with the writing.

Here's how it begins:

My sister never lets me play princess in her castle.
But that is fine. I will find my OWN castle.
And I know just where to go.

Illustrator Note: Regan goes outside and sees the garden shed.

I tiptoe real quiet to the window,
*   peek inside and look left . . .*
*   and right . . .*

Illustrator Note: Regan sees
gnomes in the garden shed.

"TRESPASSERS!"
I shout and spring away from the ledge.
*   I can't go into that castle without an army of knights.*
Gnomes steal little girls' hair for their beards!
*   This is NOT my castle. I will have to find another.*

Illustrator Note: A toad hops by in front of Regan.

Hop,
*   Hop,*
*   Hop.*

"STOP TOAD!"

*   If I catch him, I can turn him*
*   into a prince with a kiss.*
*   Then take his castle.*

For this example, I'm using formatting to add emphasis, page turns, and voice. Note that capitalization is used to represent shouting.

This time, ellipses are used to make the reader pause, and I added extra indentations to show movement and action in the story. Each action—tiptoeing, peeking, looking—is broken into its own line for emphasis. You can use this technique to highlight separate actions in your story.

You'll also notice I added illustrator notes to this manuscript. Because it's told in first person, I wanted to keep Regan's voice unique and rely on illustrations to show some things in the story, like the garden shed and the toad. We'll talk about illustrator notes in Chapter Seven, but when used well, they can also add interest to your manuscript.

Adding in Back Matter

The final thing that can help you improve your manuscript is back matter. This is the information that appears at the end of some books that can also help during the editing process.

What is back matter?

Back matter is anything included at the back of the book that connects to the story but isn't a part of the story itself. It's really great to include when you have a nonfiction book but can also be included if you want to discuss a specific topic, value, or theme in a fiction book.

Types of back matter:

While back matter can come in many different formats, these are some of the most popular kinds you might find in a picture book:

- Author's Note

- Discussion Questions

- Activity Instructions

- Recipe Guide

- Fun Facts

- Additional Links or Further **Reading**

You can also consider including this to help make your story more marketable to a publisher, and eventually to librarians and teachers. But before you do that, I find it helpful during the editing process.

Because so many of us have very meaningful messages and ideas for stories, our writing can sometimes come across as "didactic." This is an industry term for a book that focuses too heavily on teaching or moral instruction, and it is something that you want to avoid at all costs.

If you're struggling with the pace of your story—it feels slow or you aren't sure how to include your message without being didactic—consider incorporating back matter. By putting your message focus here, you can open up the story to be more fun, entertaining, or engaging for young readers.

Examples of books with back matter:

- *Oh, My! It's a Dragonfly!* by Carla Burke (BiblioKid Publishing, 2024)

- *Tag! You're It* by Jannesy DeLeon (BiblioKid Publishing, 2022)

- *When We Are Apart* by Becca Johnsey (BiblioKid Publishing, 2023)

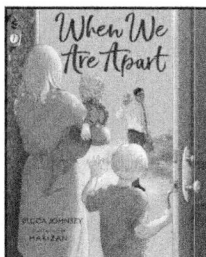

Spend time working through the edits of your manuscript before you jump into the next chapter. Use the Kidlit Editing Checklist found in your workbook. (If you haven't downloaded it yet, you can get it free at JourneytoKidlit.com/PBP-Free-Resources.)

ACTION STEP:

Complete the Chapter Activity.

Get the Kidlit Editing Checklist inside the Companion Workbook.

Download it at JourneytoKidlit.com/PBP-Free-Resources if you haven't already.

CHAPTER SEVEN

The Illustrator's Role in Picture Books

LIKE MANY new writers, I thought about illustrating my book when I wrote my first manuscript. (I was a decent enough artist and then wouldn't have to split the royalties. It made sense to me.)

However, when I first started out, I didn't understand the true role of an illustrator. I thought that if I could at least create the initial sketches, it would give a publisher an idea of what I was visualizing because I thought they'd need to "see" the book to fully understand my vision.

Have you had a similar thought—for someone to enjoy your story, they'd need to see the entire book to truly "get it"?

As someone who coaches thousands of writers per month, I know that a lot of people believe you need illustrations to feel connected to the story. Or they think the story won't be great without illustrations. Or a reader won't be able to understand it or feel connected to it because it doesn't have the illustrations yet.

No matter what you're thinking, I want you to know first and foremost that your manuscript needs to be great on its own without illustrations. It's not the illustrator's job to do all the heavy lifting for you. Make sure your manuscript is truly publishing-ready before moving onto this step—you do this by completing all the action steps in Chapter Five and Chapter Six first.

> **Pro Tip:** Have your manuscript critiqued by either a professional or skilled peer critique group when you think it's "finished." At the end of this book, you can find a link to help you get a critique.

Okay, trusting that you'll have a great story, let's chat about when to find an illustrator and if you need to find one yourself.

Whose Job is it to Find an Illustrator?

This is a two-part answer because it depends on how you plan to publish your children's book.

- If you plan to **self-publish your picture book,** you'll need to find an illustrator. Although there are many different places to find an illustrator, I suggest checking freelancing sites, like Behance or Upwork, because they have various styles to fit a range of budgets.

- But if you want to work with a **traditional publisher,** most of the time, you won't have to find an illustrator. The publishing house will find someone they feel is best suited to create the images for your book. (Sometimes, you'll be able to give your input on who they choose, and other times, the publisher will choose for you.)

※ · ※ · ✹ · ※ · ※

Should You Submit Your Story with Illustrations?

This question often comes up with new writers, and I completely understand where it's coming from. As someone who first submitted a dummy book with my story, I know how important images can feel to help support a manuscript. However, I highly suggest you do not submit illustrations with your story.

Here's why.

1. It might be the wrong fit for the editor.

As an editor at a publishing house, I know what it's like to read a story and instantly visualize what the book will look like. Sometimes, I even have a specific portfolio pop into my mind with whom I'd like to collect a sample from.

However, if the illustrations are already included, that could cloud an editor's vision. Sometimes, it lines up; other times, it's way different. If you submit to an editor who doesn't like the illustrations but enjoys the story, they may not want to go with either, for fear you won't want to change the illustrations.

Often, if an editor likes a story but not the illustrations, they will offer to purchase the story and not the art. This can come as a blow to someone who's an author/illustrator and a bummer when it's a duo.

While writing may be a solitary process, publishing is meant to be more collaborative. If your book feels too finished or like the editor might not have space to collaborate with you on the book, then it might be easier to pass on your project and find one with more room for collaboration.

2. It might give the impression that you aren't willing or able to edit your story.

When you submit the art along with the story, the editor may also assume that this is the final vision you have in mind. If it's not theirs, they may think you aren't willing or able to edit the story or change any issues they see in the draft.

It's always devastating to me when I read a manuscript that clearly needs edits, and later learn the author has already begun working with an illustrator. Illustrations can be a significant investment, so often times, the author isn't willing or able to make the edits needed, which means we have to reject the book. And I get so sad about that because I know they're going to publish a book that isn't ready to be published. (Which means it's really going to struggle to sell.)

3. It can lead to rejection.

Instead of being an advantage, having the artwork finished ahead of time may actually work against you. In many cases, an editor who receives a submission with illustrations that encounter either of the issues above may just send a rejection letter and move on. Especially if the art's not done well or the story relies too heavily on the illustrations instead of being a well-written book.

So, if you should wait to get an illustrator, how should you prepare your manuscript for illustrations instead?

Using Illustration Notes

Yes, it's the illustrator's job to come up with all the art, but it doesn't mean you're off the hook entirely as a writer. You should still visualize your story and make sure to note any important artistic elements as needed.

For instance, *Humans In-Training* is written in first person from a dog's point of view. This means that unless I tell the reader upfront who my main character is, they could read over half the book before they understand it's a dog. That could be a very confusing reading environment for them and make it less enjoyable to read. To avoid this, all I need to do is add an illustrator note at the beginning so the reader is clued in right away.

What are illustrator notes?

Illustrator notes are comments from the author to the illustrator or reader about what they need to visualize. They are NOT, however, directions on how to draw.

For instance, in the case of *Humans In-Training*, I didn't say, "This is a golden retriever puppy with crimped ears in a yellow hue." Instead, all I said was, "From a dog's point-of-view." That way, it's just a quick note to put a visual in someone's head as they read my manuscript. The type of dog doesn't matter, and it leaves room for the illustrator to choose what to draw.

You don't want to tell the illustrator exactly what to draw because you want them to bring an added element of creativity and voice to the story. That's why at a traditional publishing house, authors and illustrators typically don't communicate with each other. Publishers want the illustrator to feel free to express themselves.

Even if you plan to self-publish your book, I would still allow the illustrator room to breathe and bring their own spin to the story. If it fits your vision and expectations for the book's quality, it's great. And who knows, you might be pleasantly surprised to see how much better their idea is than yours.

When to include illustrator notes:

It's honestly hard to begin writing for kids when you're only exposed to picture books as the finished product. After seeing these fully illustrated books, it can be tempting to think you need to add a lot of description or dictate exactly what needs to be drawn for the person reading your manuscript to understand what you're trying to convey.

However, in a professional environment, most writers use very few illustrator notes or only include notes with a very intentional purpose. This is something I want you to work toward, too. Below are the five best guidelines for using illustrator notes (and when to rework your story instead).

Do: include them when what you wrote can't be visualized without an explanation.

This doesn't mean to move all descriptions you had removed from your text in the editing stage to illustrator notes. Like I said before, it's not the author's job to tell the illustrator exactly what to draw. However, sometimes you might want to make up a word or incorporate something with very little context. In those types of situations, including an illustrator note can be really helpful for the reader.

For example, if I say, "He shot the zombie pickles with

his snortblat," I may need a brief illustrator note to explain what a snortblat looks like if its use is integral to the story. (If the working mechanics aren't required, the note might not be needed either.)

Another example would be if I use a repeating sound like "Beep, Beep, Beep" but don't include any context to go with the sound; I might want to include a quick illustrator note that says, "Truck is backing up." As the writer, your goal should be to keep the reader invested in your story, so use your best judgment on when to pull them out with a brief aside using an illustrator note.

Don't: use them as a way to describe exactly what you picture.

I know it seems like this might have already been mentioned, but I see so many stories with long paragraphs of illustrator notes. This is exactly what not to do. If your picture book word count is too high, please don't move everything to be an illustrator note. Instead, go back through the previous chapters and find ways to tell a better story first.

To help, think about each of your notes as something that yanks the reader out of the story. You don't want to have an illustrator note after each line because that will give your reader whiplash trying to get through it, and unless you've paid them to read your story, they're more likely to stop reading. Avoid that by limiting the number of times you pull the reader out of the story. And remember, not all editors or agents read illustrator notes in their first read-through, so if all your important story information is in the notes, they could miss a lot of what's happening in your story.

Do: leave room for the illustrator to interpret their own ideas.

I've mentioned this before, but an illustrator is a creative person who is here to add value and voice to your story. (Their own perspective and voice, that is.) If you tell them exactly what to draw to the minute detail and pick every color, you're taking away the joy they receive from getting to create illustrations. As I tell all the authors I work with, if it doesn't change the story or directly impact the plot, then it doesn't need a note.

This is important to keep in mind both as you write the book and as you get the first look at sketches. If you care too much about controlling things that don't matter to the overall story—like whether a backpack is blue or purple when a backpack isn't even mentioned—then you have a higher chance of slowing the production process, delaying the publication date of your book, and ending a relationship with an illustrator. All things you want to avoid.

Don't: put descriptions in the story to help the illustrations make sense.

The opposite of putting everything in the illustrator notes is putting it all in the story. But if you're doing your picture book practice as you should be, you'll notice that most professional picture book authors use very limited language yet still convey big ideas. (Check out the reading list in your workbook for books to read and type out for reference if you haven't started doing this yet.) You can use the previous chapters to help you cut unnecessary text or submit your manuscript for a critique for help knowing where to cut.

Do: use them as many times as needed, as long as you're following the other rules.

The final note is that there isn't a hard rule for the number of illustration notes you need. Instead, that will be determined by your writing style and how you plan to use the illustrations for your story. Just be sure to go back through the previous rules to make sure you're not misusing your illustration notes or giving your reader whiplash by including a note after every line in your story.

ILLUSTRATOR NOTES CHEAT SHEET

ILLUSTRATOR NOTES–DO LIST

- Do include them when what you wrote can't be visualized without an explanation.
- Do leave room for the illustrator to interpret their own ideas.
- Do use them as many times as needed in order to tell the full story, as long as you're following the other rules.

ILLUSTRATOR NOTES–DON'T LIST

- Don't use them as a way to describe exactly what you picture.
- Don't put descriptions in the story to help the illustrations make sense.
- Don't use them between every line to try to get the reader to visualize every single page exactly like you do.

Choosing your illustrator:

If you are still considering illustrating your own story, the best rule of thumb is to walk down the picture book aisle and look at illustrations. Ask yourself, "Would my illustrations stack up to the illustrations in these books?" Looking back at my own submission all those years ago, the sketches and quality of art were nowhere near what a reader would expect to purchase.

Don't let the idea of having someone illustrate your book scare you. Trained children's book illustrators will actually improve on your words and help you complete a better book than you'd originally imagined. This should give you peace to let go of that aspect of control, knowing that someone out there will do this better than you could.

Your goal should always be to bring the highest quality book to the marketplace that children will want to read again and again. If that means having a publisher help select an illustrator for you instead of being an author-illustrator yourself or waiting a little longer to hire an illustrator so you have enough budget to hire the person you really want to, that's okay.

For now, start thinking about the illustrations that might appear in your book and use the picture book layout to see how the story paginates. We'll discuss what to do once you have a finished manuscript in the next chapter.

ACTION STEP:

TO DO!

Complete the Chapter Activity.

Get the <u>Picture Book Page Layout</u> inside the Companion Workbook.

Download it at JourneytoKidlit.com/PBP-Free-Resources if you haven't already.

CHAPTER EIGHT

Finishing Your Manuscript

CONGRATULATIONS! You've finally finished writing your children's book. (Or you will soon.)

I finished my first picture book in a month, showed it to my mom and best friend, and then Googled places to send it. However, after sending it to the first five publishers or agencies I could find and hearing crickets back, I met a woman at my church writing group who helped set me straight on the "publishing" process.

It's now my turn to be that guide for you.

You see, that first book I wrote was nowhere close to publishing-ready, even though I thought it was finished. So, before you make the same mistake I made by moving as quickly as possible to the publishing process, I want you to complete these steps first. (Trust me, it'll save you a lot of embarrassment and rejection in the long run.)

What to Do When You've Finished

Once you have a finished draft, there are three main things that you should do first.

1. Determine your writing goals.

This is a step that many writers skip, but it's the key to knowing where to publish your children's book. This industry is competitive, and, if you're not careful, it can be really disheartening as you get started.

Before you choose how you want to start, really think about what you want to accomplish with your book. Ask yourself:

- Why do you want to publish a children's book?

- What are the most important parts of your book that you're not willing to compromise?

- What would you like to do once you have a children's book out?

Depending on how you answer those questions will help you as you move on to the next chapter and choose the publishing path for you.

2. Write your winning hook.

No matter what publishing option you choose, you need a hook that will set your book apart. Your hook will be the pitch you'll use to attract either publishers or parents to your book and make them want to read it. We'll go over pitching in detail in the next chapter.

3. Make sure your story's truly "publishing-ready."

As a publisher, most of the manuscripts I read are not ready to be published. They often still need a lot of edits. Whether or not you plan on trying to publish your book with a publisher, your story still needs to be a polished piece that's ready for publication. Before you submit or try to publish your story yourself, you must make sure it's absolutely ready to publish as a children's book. The best way to do this is to have it critiqued.

It's also important to note that while I had my mom and friend read my story, they were not qualified critique partners. Instead, your friends and family are beta readers, meaning they're only qualified to give you their opinion from a reader's perspective since they don't understand the writing techniques required for children's books.

Make sure to only take manuscript edits from a skilled peer critique group who also studies children's book writing or a children's book writing professional when seeking feedback. Here's how you can get started finding someone to review your manuscript.

Finding a Critique Group

It's vital that you have your story reviewed by an industry professional or a critique group of other writers who are specifically writing children's books. Otherwise, you risk sending something that's not ready for publishing to an agent or editor, which will only get you a rejection letter. Or self-publishing something that will struggle to sell, leaving you disappointed with the results. (And I want to help you avoid as much heartache as possible during the publishing process!)

Here are some of the best ways I recommend to find either critique partners or professionals to review your manuscript . . .

- **Join Kidlit Academy** to get access to our private Facebook community. Here, we host monthly peer critiques for our students to get feedback on their pages.

- **Sign up for a written critique from the Journey to Kidlit editing team.** We provide you with a Story Seal-of-Approval rating to help you know how close your story is to being "publishing-ready."

- **Check with your local library.** Libraries like to host events, including writer meet-ups. Visit your local library's website for upcoming events, or talk to a librarian to see if they offer this.

- **Ask the Regional Advisor of your SCBWI Region (The Society of Children's Book Writers and Illustrators).** They should have a list of monthly activities they have available for members and can help you connect with others who are looking for a critique group.

- **Connect with others on social media** who may also want to form a critique group. Just make sure they write picture books, too. And set up a system for what's expected from the members to make it worth everyone's time.

Alternatively, you can form a critique group yourself if you know a handful of other children's book writers who want to receive feedback.

Forming a critique group:

I've had the same critique group for a decade now, and I wouldn't have succeeded without them. They've read every version of my manuscripts, from the most polished to the roughest first drafts, and they're always honest about what needs to be improved before I consider something "finished." They're also some of my best friends in the writing community. I highly recommend you find your own core group of writers you can work with through this process.

When forming your own critique group, remember that everyone must find value from the group and that you're not just attending for the benefit of your own story. In order to make sure everyone gets something out of your group, here are my suggestions on how to host a strong meeting.

1. Have a regular monthly meeting time.

When you have a set time each month that works for the group, this will keep you consistent both with your writing times and your critiques. (Having a monthly critique deadline used to be the only reason I found time to write when I first started.) Find a time that works for everyone and commit to it.

2. Make sure all stories are submitted in advance.

This not only ensures people are accountable for bringing things to the group, but it also allows time to review the stories in advance. For example, my group usually has a deadline of the day before so we have at least 24 hours to read something, but you can decide what will work best for your group.

3. Take turns letting each person share their thoughts for each story being critiqued.

It's no fun if one person dominates the whole discussion in anything, especially critiques. This is also really important when you're new because you might not feel confident that you can give good critiques yet. However, by forcing yourself to do this monthly, you'll improve your skills on what to look for to help improve other people's children's book manuscripts and become a better writer yourself.

If the idea of giving feedback intimidates you because you're not confident in your writing skills, please note that you're still a reader. As a reader, you're able to express when you find something confusing or if something tripped you up as you were reading. You might not know how to fix things yet, but letting them know where you experienced these issues is very helpful to the other writer. I also recommend everyone follow the "Sandwich Method" when giving feedback.

4. Use the "Sandwich Method" for Your Critiques.

The "Sandwich Method" is a great way to ensure everyone receives positive feedback along with helpful notes. This is really important too if you're new to giving feedback or hesitant to share your writing with others for fear of negative feedback.

✳ · ✳ · ✵ · ✳ · ✳

THE
SANDWICH METHOD

1. Start with something positive.

2. Focus on the big picture.
Where are some spots you were tripped up?
Where are the confusing parts?
What needs the most attention?

3. End with some words of encouragement
or additional positive notes
about things you liked.

How to give feedback using the sandwich method:

- Start with something positive. (Highlight the parts of the story you enjoyed.)

- Focus on the big picture. Where are some spots you were tripped up? Where are the confusing parts? What needs the most attention?

- You can also add notes on sentence structure/grammar/etc., if it's a pretty polished piece, but it's not required or necessary if you're suggesting big picture changes first.
- End with some words of encouragement or additional positive notes about things you liked.

Writing groups are also a fantastic resource for asking questions and having a dedicated group of friends to share your ups and your downs with. There will be a lot of them along your writing journey!

If you don't have a group yet, I highly recommend you prioritize finding one that works for you. Join Kidlit Academy at JourneytoKidlit.com/Signup-KL-Academy to get access to our private Facebook community for monthly accountability, peer critiques, and a space to network with other children's book writers.

Getting the "Green" Light to Move Forward

When I started writing, my biggest question was always: "How do I know if my story is ready to move forward?" Because I wanted to get published fast! Normally, I would already be picturing my finished book before I'd even written a first draft.

Maybe that's you, too, and you're wondering how quickly you can get published. Well, at Journey to Kidlit, we have a simple way of knowing . . .

How to know if you're ready to get published:

I call it the "Story Seal of Approval." And it's the rating system we use at Journey to Kidlit for an author to easily know if their story is ready to send to agents or publishers.

When you send your story for critique, think about the notes you receive on a scale from one to three.

1. **Time for Edits:** Your story has big-picture issues that need to be resolved before you tighten and polish it for publication.

2. **Great Start:** The story components are mostly there, but you need to tighten and line edit the story before preparing it for publication.

3. **Story Approved:** This story is solid, and with a strong pitch, should be ready to begin querying.

Keeping this rating system in mind will help you avoid the number one mistake new writers make when trying to get published. That's submitting a story too soon and trying to rush the publishing process.

Like I said before, when I was first starting out, I was so excited about my story idea and couldn't wait for it to be a book. I knew it was something that was not only needed in the market, but would also sell once it was published.

I thought I just needed to get it in front of a publisher.

Which is what you might be thinking, too. If only you could

get your story in front of a publisher, then they'll know how to make your dream happen. But before you do what I did—send your story to a list of publishers and agents without understanding the process—I want you to pump the brakes.

This is **the #1 reason most stories get rejected**, so please resist moving forward too soon. In order to know if your story's truly ready to be published, you need to first have it reviewed by someone who knows the industry. (You can still have your mom and best friend as beta readers, but remember, they can't give you manuscript feedback from an editorial perspective.)

Professional reviewers and skilled critique partners will let you know if your story:

- Will resonate with readers
- Is ready to send to publishers

Make sure you don't skip this step. If you'd like to book a written critique with the Journey to Kidlit editing team, visit JourneytoKidlit.com/Book-Critique-Session. Once you've officially gotten the "green light" from either a professional editor or your critique group, then it's time to move on to the next chapter—and my favorite step—having your book published.

ACTION STEP:

Complete the Chapter Activity.

Get the <u>Publishing Ready Checklist</u> inside the Companion Workbook.

Download it at JourneytoKidlit.com/PBP-Free-Resources if you haven't already.

CHAPTER NINE

Getting Your Book Published

INALLY, IT'S TIME to talk about how to publish your children's book! I don't know about you, but as soon as I have an idea, I always think about getting it published. I picture myself reading to a group of kids at the school down the street from my house, and walking into Barnes and Noble and seeing my book on the shelf next to the other picture books.

When this finally happened for me, it was everything I'd dreamed of and more. I'm excited to help you get published, too.

Before you officially begin the publishing process, take off your writer hat, and put on your marketing hat. No matter how you plan on getting published, you need to know how to sell your book. And it all starts with your pitch.

Writing Your Pitch

Your pitch is used to help you sell your book to either a publisher or a reader. It's important to get this right. In previous chapters, I've hinted at knowing your hook or pitch for your book, but in this section, we'll dive into how to write an effective pitch.

An effective pitch will connect the reader to your story and give them a reason to care, but it doesn't reveal the whole story.

Instead, it gives them just enough to pique their interest and get them asking for more. You don't want to take up too much of the reader's time with this because the goal is to get them to the story and to begin reading the pages.

Two things to include in your pitch:

There are two critical key ingredients in a good pitch that you should plan to include. The first is WHO is the story about? And second, WHAT is at stake for them? What's your story's main goal or focus, and what's standing in the character's way of reaching that goal?

You've already done a lot of the foundational work for this in the earlier chapters when you were gathering your story assets, so you should know this information. However, it's important to note that the *what* in the pitch should be reserved for your external goal, not your internal goal.

Pitch formula to use:

This is the most common formula to use when writing a pitch for your book: {Title of Story} is about {Main Character} who must {action they take} in order to {achieve their goal}.

Don't rush to fill in the blanks with this. Instead, take time brainstorming multiple answers. Your goal should be to write something that will spark a reader's curiosity. You don't want to be vague or boring. So, focus on being **very specific** about the situation in your book. That's the secret sauce to standing out.

Do not focus solely on the theme or message that you're trying to portray. Great pitches will use the internal goal to help solidify why someone would want to purchase the book. But remember, you don't have a plot without an external goal. Your external goal should be the focus of your pitch.

To help you better understand how to be creative with writing your idea, I have some examples of pitches from recently published books by BiblioKid Publishing.

Examples of picture book pitches:

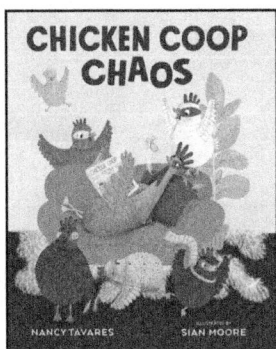

1. *Chicken Coop Chaos*
by Nancy Tavares
(BiblioKid Publishing, 2023)

Pearl liked the peace and order of her henhouse. So when Wendell, a rooster, tries to move in, she squawks to kick him out right away. But he only crosses his wings and refuses to leave. Can Pearl hatch a plan to get him to leave? Or will she be forced to live in a chicken coop of chaos? Find out in this rollicking read-aloud by debut author, Nancy Tavares.

2. *Connor Wants His Old House Back* by Donna Downing (BiblioKid Publishing, 2024)

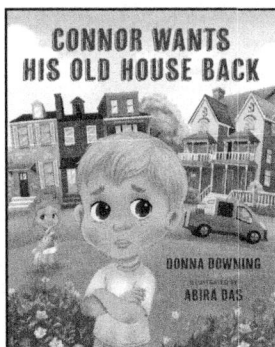

When Connor is faced with moving to a new house, he finds everything wrong with it. He really does not want to move. Everything seems wrong. But he quickly discovers that all the differences between the two houses also have a lot of positives!

3. *Oh, My! It's a Dragonfly!* by Carla Burke (BiblioKid Publishing, 2024)

A tiny egg at the bottom of the pond is about to hatch. What is hidden inside? Go on this action-packed adventure and learn the life cycle of a dragonfly in this engaging picture book.

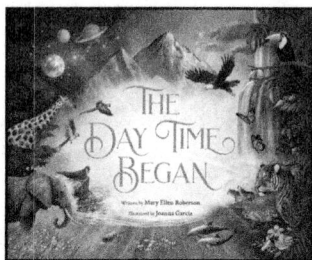

4. *The Day Time Began* by Mary Ellen Roberson (BiblioKid Publishing, 2024)

Go back to the beginning—before there was time. THE DAY TIME BEGAN is a lively and lyrical retelling of the story of creation. With over 160 different kinds of realistically illustrated animals to discover, this picture book is sure to excite pre-school through second grade children about God's greatness and the wonders of His marvelous creation.

5. *Tiki Tim* by Madison Caputi (BiblioKid Publishing, 2024)

When a young surfer's wish leads to a beachside tiki mysteriously coming to life, the unlikely duo find themselves diving into all of the wonderful things that Adventure Bay has to offer. But as they quickly discover, the best parts of life aren't created by the things we do, but by the friends we do them with. TIKI TIM is an intriguing, fun, anytime picture book that celebrates friendship, new adventures, and wishes coming true.

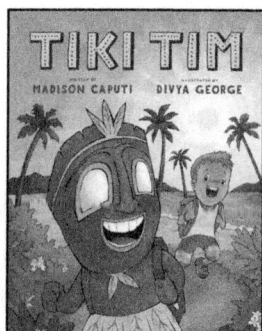

As you can see, each of these books has different characters, themes, and plots, but they all follow a similar structure when explaining what the book is about to pique a reader's interest. Give it a try using your own idea!

PRO TIP: Use the Pitch Sheet in your workbook to help you as you work on this. If you haven't already, you can download it at JourneytoKidlit.com/PBP-Free-Resources to get started.

Your Three Publishing Options

Now that you know what you're selling and how you're going to sell it, it's time to figure out how to get published. At Journey to Kidlit, we have a big mission to help get 100,000 books written by authors of all different backgrounds, experiences, and locations onto bookshelves in the next ten years.

We don't care how you get published; we just care that you do.

There are three publishing options for authors: traditional publishing, self-publishing, and hybrid publishing. While you may know a little about each, you might still be unsure which is best for you or how to get started. So, let's break it down.

1. Traditional Publishing

Traditional Publishing is the oldest option and normally the first option authors think of when they want to publish their book. And for good reason! It's beneficial to have someone help you with the process. But it's not required.

PUBLISHING OPTIONS

TRADITIONAL	SELF	HYBRID
Expert Help with Process	No Help or Hired Expert Help	Expert Help with Process
No or Minimal Upfront Costs	Full Cost of Production Upfront	Full Cost of Production Upfront
Time to Publication Average 2-3 Years	Time to Publication Average < 1 Year	Time to Publication Average < 1 Year

The Pros to Traditional Publishing:

One of the biggest benefits of traditional publishing is having a team of experienced people helping you create your book. They will find the illustrator, determine the layout, absorb all the costs, and assist in the marketing and distribution of the book. (The amount is determined by the publisher.)

This is AWESOME, especially if you're trying to make a great book but don't have the means to do it yourself. It's also nice to have a team of professionals to help guide you along the way, especially when you're new to the industry and may not be sure about everything you need to do in order to publish a book. I have a complete list of publishers and agencies who specialize in children's books called the Kidlit Insider. You can find it inside Kidlit Academy if you'd like help getting a traditional publishing contract.

The Cons to Traditional Publishing:

While there are many benefits to traditional publishing, it wouldn't be fair if we didn't also talk about the negatives of working with a traditional publisher. One of which is time.

Since there's relatively no risk to an author with this publishing path, there's A LOT of competition, which means it could take a while before you get a yes. (A common rule of thumb in the industry is between five to ten years before you get your first publishing contract with a traditional publisher—while some may be able to do it faster, this is the average time expectancy.)

Another downside to traditional publishing is control. When you give your book to a publisher, you also give up control and almost all say over what happens with your book. This varies by publisher and should be considered before signing a contract.

The publisher may have the final say on:

- The illustrator and layout of the book
- The title and certain writing elements of the story
- The marketing and how much or little they want to contribute

If this gives you pause, go back to the goals for your book and your reasons for publishing that you listed in the previous chapter. If your character absolutely MUST be a specific way and you couldn't imagine changing your story for anyone, then maybe self-publishing or hybrid publishing might be a better option for you.

2. Self-Publishing

With self-publishing, you'll do all the work that a traditional publisher would handle, but on your own. This includes edits, illustrations, book design, print, distribution, and marketing. But just because the word "self" is in the name, it doesn't mean you have to do everything alone. You can always hire professionals to help you along the process.

The Pros to Self-Publishing:

One of the big advantages of self-publishing is that you can move quickly. You can finish your book in a few months or within a year and have it ready for publication. It's all up to you.

As the publisher, you can also decide what your book looks like. What will the title be? How will the pacing work? What kind of illustrations do you want? Who do you want to work with? You have complete control, which is wonderful. Plus, investing upfront let's you earn more once the book is listed for sale.

Cons to Self-Publishing:

One of the downsides of self-publishing is the same as its advantage—it's all on you. You're the publisher, so you have to stay organized, manage the budget, make sure the book gets finished, give notes to the illustrator, find the printer and distributor, and handle marketing. And you have to tell people that your book exists!

As a new author, you might feel overwhelmed and imposter syndrome or fear can creep in. You might second-guess whether your book is good enough or if it's the right time to publish. It's important to know yourself and what you're capable of handling.

If you're interested in self-publishing, check out printers like Amazon KDP or IngramSpark. These are great, user-friendly options, and they're fast. If your budget is tight, you can always learn how to do some of these tasks yourself. You can learn how to create the final files, PDFs, and EPUBs. It's possible but will take time, so there's a trade-off. You'll either spend money or time—it's up to you.

Just be sure not to sacrifice quality for budget or time. It's better to create an amazing book over the course of many years than to rush to print it and feel disappointed by the end product.

Remember, no matter which option you choose, you're still a published author. You can still do school visits, book signings, and other activities whether you traditionally publish or self-publish. The choice you make doesn't make you any less of an author.

3. Hybrid Publishing

Our third and final option is hybrid publishing. Hybrid publishing has become increasingly popular for writers because of its quick turnarounds and high amount of author control, but how do you know if this is the right choice for you and your story?

The Pros to Hybrid Publishing:

A hybrid publisher aims to combine the help and support of a traditional publishing house while giving the author complete control of the end product. However, not all hybrids do this in the same way.

There are some who help you after the final files are complete. Also considered a self-publishing service, these houses will help you print your book and get it into distribution. If you choose this type of publisher, you will first need to find an illustrator and editor to help you finish your story before working with them—much like when you're self-publishing.

On the other hand, some hybrid publishers will help you create those final files. These are full-service hybrid publishers, which means they help with the complete publishing process—editing, finding an illustrator, designing the book, printing, distributing, and marketing. Some offer package deals for you to choose from at different price levels, while others are all-inclusive—walking you through each step of the process as a team for a set price.

The Cons to Hybrid Publishing:

For some authors, the biggest drawback to using a hybrid publisher is the upfront investment. Contrary to traditional publishing, which requires almost zero monetary investment outside of learning the craft of writing, a hybrid publisher requires a monetary contribution from you.

Self-publishing also involves a monetary investment from the writer; however, you usually have more control over the budget and can make it more cost-effective if necessary.

On average, a hybrid publisher could cost between $8,000-$12,000 to publish your book. (Some may be more or less depending on the services they offer.) The reason for this significant investment can be due to the number of services included or the quantity of books printed for you.

Make sure to always do your research when searching for a hybrid publisher. It can sometimes be hard to know which companies are truly legitimate and which ones may be hard or challenging to work with. I always suggest setting up a call to discuss your book before selecting a publisher to ensure you know what you're entering into before signing a contract.

A Hybrid Publisher just for Children's Books:

If you're interested in hybrid publishing, I recommend BiblioKid Publishing. This American hybrid publishing house focuses solely on publishing books for kids ages 0 to 8. Plus, they can even work with international authors! You can learn more about them at submissions.bibliokidpublishing.com.

No matter which option you choose, just note that publishing a children's book can be a long and daunting process. (Trust me. It took me five years before I saw my first book in print.)

While it can sometimes be tiring or frustrating, nothing compares to finally holding your book in your hands. The first time you hear a child reading, it is enough to make your heart melt and forget all the struggle it took to get there. If you start feeling overwhelmed, relax and take a breath. It's your journey. Take it as slow or as fast as you want to.

Before we conclude this book, I want to share some additional resources to help you. They are in the next chapter. See you there!

ACTION STEP:

TO DO!

Complete the Chapter Activity.

Get the Manuscript Pitch Prep worksheet inside the Companion Workbook.

Download it at JourneytoKidlit.com/PBP-Free-Resources if you haven't already.

CHAPTER TEN

What's Next?

CONGRATULATIONS! You've made it to the final chapter in the book. Thanks so much for sticking with me.

As you continue forward on your Kidlit journey, it's important to remember that writing is a form of art. Like with every other art form, not everyone will like what you create. But that doesn't make your story any less impressive. It just means it's not someone's taste.

This is especially true when you're trying to traditionally publish your book because you'll start by receiving lots of rejection letters and some that say it's not a fit. When that happens, don't take it personally. A 'no' doesn't mean start over; it just means move on to the next.

It's also important to remember that this is a business. If someone rejects your story, it's not personal; it's business. Send it to more people to review, then revise and submit it again.

If your book doesn't sell right away or you get a bad review, consider that happens in every business. Just keep marketing and pushing your book, and if you have to, take a marketing class. (I have a course called Kidlit Launch School to help you if needed.)

No matter what, don't give up!

You're a writer for a reason, and your book serves a purpose. Remember, at Journey to Kidlit, we strongly believe every picture book deserves a space on a child's bookshelf if you can write it well enough. That's why we're on a mission to add 100,000 new books to shelves in the next ten years.

Keep working on the topics we discussed in this book, and eventually, you'll get to hold your own published picture book in your hands.

Until next time, happy writing!

Brooke Van Sickle

Owner and Founder | Journey to Kidlit

Follow me on Instagram @JourneytoKidlit for more children's book writing tips.

Get the Picture Book Reading List

As you know, the number one way to know what is selling in today's market is to read recently published books. Throughout this book, I mentioned various picture books that you should read. You can find the complete list in the workbook.

If you haven't already, download it for free at JourneytoKidlit. com/PBP-Free-Resources. Then, use the free workbook to help you study recently published books and find your own writing voice.

Join the Kidlit Community

While I tried to put every bit of information as possible into this book, let's be honest . . . you might still have questions. How do you know if it's good enough? Or that it's really ready to be published? Writing a book can also be a very lonely process. Without a network of other writers to encourage and motivate you, it can be tempting to push your book to the back burner. And I don't want either of those things to be the reason you give up on your book.

Your story idea is **meant to be published**. (We believe that firmly here at Journey to Kidlit. So much so, that it's the mission behind all we do.) And we want to make it easy for you!

That's why I created Kidlit Academy, a live program for you to connect with industry leaders and feel supported as you finish your children's book. It includes video lessons and real-life examples of everything we discussed in the book but on a deeper level. Plus, you can join me live on Zoom twice a month to get direct answers to your questions.

If that sounds like exactly what you need, and you're ready to join a community of people who understand the passion you have for your story idea, visit JourneytoKidlit.com/Signup-KL-Academy to join before our next live event.

Have Your Story Professionally Reviewed

As I mentioned throughout this book, you want to publish a children's book that you'll be proud to share with your friends and family, but it can be hard to know when it's finished. Even if you've had your family and friends read your rough draft, they might not know what it takes to write a children's book, so how can you know for sure that it doesn't need to be edited again?

The only way to know is by having someone who knows how to write and edit children's books critique your story. If you skip this step, you're more likely to get stuck in the publishing cycle so many writers find themselves in. The cycle of sending your story to publisher after publisher only to receive rejection letter after rejection letter. Which can only leave you feeling frustrated by the process and have you doubting your abilities to get published.

That is not where you want to be.

This is why I've created the "Story Seal of Approval" rating system at Journey to Kidlit. Our three-tier critique rating is designed to help you know exactly where you're at in the writing process so you can move on to the publishing process with confidence.

When you're ready to have your manuscript reviewed, book a critique at JourneytoKidlit.com/Book-Critique-Session to be paired with a member of our editing team. Once received, we'll evaluate your story's character, plot, voice, marketing potential, and any issues to focus on before you begin submissions. Use the link to save your spot today.

> NOTE: All Kidlit Academy students also receive a 20 percent discount on critiques they can use every month. You'll get the code after you sign up. Grab it from the course portal before using the link to book your critique.

We're looking forward to supporting you in anyway we can as you finish your children's book.

Liked this book? Share it with a friend.

It's proven that your chances of success are higher when you have an accountability partner. If you got value from this book and know someone else who might too, share it with them. Then, chat about it. Together, you can work toward your own publishing journeys.

I'm cheering for you.

Brooke

———◦◦◇◦◦———

Get the free BONUS chapter about
How to Write a Successful Series when you leave a review.
Email us a Screenshot of Your Review at
hello@journeytokidlit.com to get it.

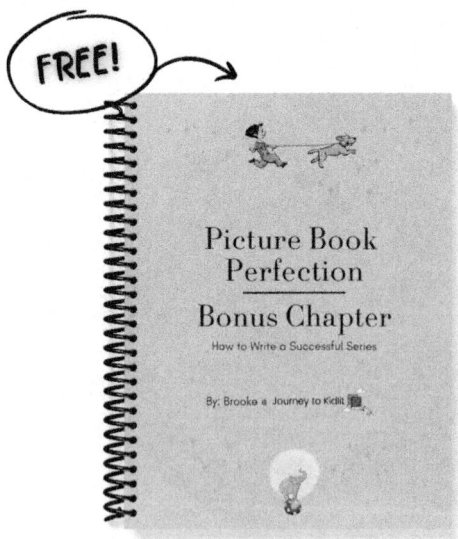

About the Author

BROOKE VAN SICKLE is the owner and founder of Journey to Kidlit, the online educational platform that teaches thousands of aspiring children's book writers from over 35 countries around the world about how to write and publish a children's book based on her own award-winning writing journey. She's also the owner of BiblioKid Publishing, an American hybrid publishing house that specializes in producing quality books for kids.

Named a 2023 Top Writing Coach by Coach Foundation, Brooke has published over 50 titles that have gone on to receive 5-star reviews from children's book publication sites like Readers' Favorite, Readers' Choice, and Mom's Choice. She's also an award-winning picture book author herself, and her book, *This Is My Castle*, received the 2020 Distinguished Favorite Preschool Picture Book Award.

When not writing or teaching, Brooke enjoys spending time with her three leading men: Mitch, Quill, and Brandon, their golden retriever.

DON'T FORGET . . .
GET THE WORKBOOK

Complete the Guided Activities that go along with this book
using the <u>FREE</u> Companion Workbook.
Download it at JourneytoKidlit.com/PBP-Free-Resources.

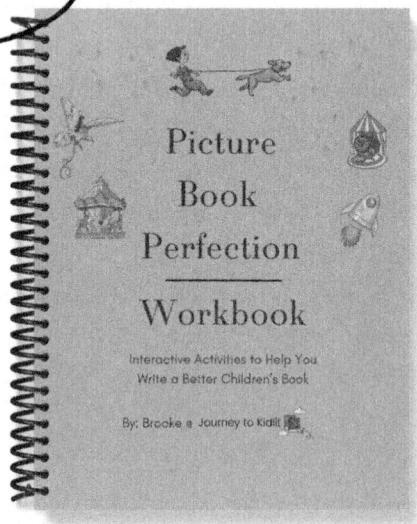

FREE!

Picture
Book
Perfection

Workbook

Interactive Activities to Help You
Write a Better Children's Book

By: Brooke ● Journey to Kidlit

Printed in Great Britain
by Amazon

58514183R00086